I0618686

TWISTED LOVE

TWISTED LOVE

MARK TRYON

CUTTING EDGE

Copyright © 1960 by Mark Tryon

The characters and events portrayed in this book are fictitious. Any similarity to real persons, living or dead, is coincidental and not intended by the author. No part of this book may be reproduced, or stored in a retrieval system, or transmitted in any form or by any means, electronic, mechanical, photocopying, recording, or otherwise, without express written permission of the publisher.

This book as originally published under the title *The Twisted Loves of Nym O'Sullivan*.

ISBN-13: 978-1-952138-58-4

Published by
Cutting Edge Books
PO Box 8212
Calabasas, CA 91372
www.cuttingedgebooks.com

CHAPTER ONE

Okeechee, Florida, is not a large town, as large towns go, but neither is it a particularly small town. A sprawling winter resort and retirement haven, it houses some five thousand families within six miles of the Gulf. It is anchored to the azure ocean by a palm-lined boulevard that terminates at Port Retreat, sometimes referred to as Okeechee Beach.

Okeechee is a community of successful people. Poverty is virtually nonexistent, except on Cane Hill, the strictly isolated Negro district. Everywhere else it seems to be peopled with healthy, wealthy, self-sufficient folks who—if they are not actually retired—manage to exude an air of ease and security. Even the ice cream man on the street appears to be in the business simply because as a retired mailman he can't sit still. The meters which line the streets are privileged to license virtually nothing but Cadillacs, or "Florida Fords" as they are called, to park. Most of the houses set back from the quiet, palm-bordered, sandy streets are ultramodern glass and white brick affairs with two-car garages and poincianas in rich profusion.

The natives and long-time residents of Okeechee, which sees only a moderate tourist trade, comprise an ingrown, intermarried tribe, whose tribal dress, according to sex, is either the brilliantly insane Florida sport shirt or the sun-back cotton dress in hues to match the rainbow.

Okeechee is a good town to spend three winter months in if you know the folks who know the folks who count. If you do not, you will be frozen out of town in less time than it takes you

1

to drink three daiquiris at the Bijou Bar, no matter how hot and summery the weather is.

Nym Bardolph had always hated the town. She hated the manner in which it seemed to be a closed corporation. She hated its smugness. She hated the fact that she had never managed to escape from it. She hated the ever-present gold-leaf sign on the office window which, viewed from where she was sitting in the large leather chair behind the steel desk, spelled:

NAVILLUS'O NAES
ROTLAER

She hated what the sign stood for—*Sean O'Sullivan, Realtor,* respectable citizen of good family, accepted at the country club. Annual income better than fifty thousand. Alderman. One-time Mayor of Okeechee. Member of this committee and that committee and every other committee.

She could spit on the sign. She could get right up and walk to the big plate-glass window that looked out on the cherry, sunny, brick-paved street and spit on the damned sign.

On the other hand, why should she? The sign did not tell the true story any longer. She, Nym Bardolph, was the actual Sean O'Sullivan, Realtor.

This was the goal she had struggled toward for eight long years of being Sean's wife. Now she had won and soon the sign would be changed.

She saw it before her mind's eye:

HPLODRAB MYN
ROTLAER

And then thought, unbidden, slid into her mind. Where was Sean now? What was he doing?

This was Monday morning. It was no longer ago than Friday that he had packed his bag and walked through the big living room of their home—her home—carrying the suitcase in his hand.

Nym had been standing by the big picture-window that opened on the flagstone terrace. She did not turn around when she heard him.

"Well, Nym. It's all yours now. The house, the business, everything."

In spite of the sweet taste of triumph there was a strange pain in her heart. "You don't have to leave town."

"I couldn't very well stay." There was no anger in his voice. Only a kind of sadness. As if she were a child and had somehow disappointed him.

Reflected in the window against the deep blue of the sky she saw his distinguished, graying head. "I'm not running you out."

"No, Nym. You're not running me out. But as Sean O'Sullivan I no longer exist. I am dead. I don't believe I could take sitting around and watching the rotting carcass."

"You always put things so melodramatically."

"Perhaps I do. It is hard for a man when he must suddenly face the fact that slowly over the years he has allowed himself to be emasculated. I simply can't stand the idea of remaining in the setting where it happened. There are too many memories, too many old friends who will now snicker behind their hands, too many possible situations to rub it into me."

Then they said nothing for a long while until finally he spoke again, the sadness deep in his voice. "Well, goodbye, Nym."

"Goodbye."

"If you don't mind, I should like to take the station wagon."

She laughed a harsh laugh. "Oh, you have a talent, don't you, for making me seem the lowest kind of rat."

"The station wagon?"

"Take it! Take it!" It was a shrill, agonized cry.

3

She did not turn around until she heard the car start up and fade off down the gravel drive. Then she turned slowly and walked to the long couch that faced the window. She sat down and stared out over the miraculous green of the golf course and the light gray of the cement-like trunks of the royal palms.

And she realized with a feeling of sudden nausea that the long-awaited victory was sour, disappointing.

Now it was Monday morning and Nym had entered the office—her office now—with a bravado that she did not feel.

The trim little blonde behind the secretarial desk had smiled brightly. "Good morning, Mrs. O'Sullivan."

"Good morning, Lynn."

"Where's Mr. O'Sullivan?"

"He won't be in this morning." Nym might have added *or any morning,* but she chose not to. She did not quite know why. But somehow she could not make herself admit that Sean's leaving was final and permanent.

She was deeply pulled by this feeling. This office was what she had wanted all these years. It was what she had worked for and intrigued for and bullied for and lied for and stolen for. But now that it was hers, she was assailed by doubts.

You're a fool, she told herself, and her handsome, even-featured face twisted painfully into a half-meant smile. She ran a nervous hand through the gleaming close-cropped brown curls that lay closely about her head, and turned her attention to Lynn. The little secretary was bent with almost comic intensity over her typewriter, her slender white fingers flying furiously over the keys. Nym stirred restlessly as she regarded the small childlike face and the slender figure. Her mouth grew dry and she rose from her chair and walked around Lynn to the water cooler behind the girl's back. Over the edge of the paper cup Nym observed the healthy straightness of the spine and the taut boyishness of the hips. She saw the faint line of the panties where the sitting position pulled the thin summer dress tightly against the rounded thighs.

A shuddering sigh found its way into her throat and the hand that held the paper cup trembled.

Why not? The thought went through her head like searing flame. Why not? For eight years I have controlled it so that there should be never a mark against me. But now I am free. Now I am my own mistress.

She thought briefly of Sean and the hunger grew in her, grew and grew.

"Lynn..." She was amazed and a little frightened to realize that her voice was hoarse and shook with ill-concealed desire. "I'm going to the inner office. I am taking over for Mr. O'Sullivan for a while. He...he's gone on a vacation." Why *couldn't* she make herself say that he was gone for good? That she had driven him out? "There... there are some letters I want you to take. Lock the front door so we won't be disturbed and come in there with your notebook, will you?"

"Of course, Mrs. O'Sullivan."

Nym left the front room rapidly, her knees shaking as she walked. She was gripped by a dreadful excitement. An excitement that turned her stomach to jelly and her knees to rubber. She had trouble breathing. Her mouth felt hot and dry.

How long had she been wanting the small blonde girl? Now, when Nym thought back, it seemed as if the desire had been latent in her from the moment she had seen Lynn two years before when she had come, fresh from business college, to work for Sean.

The inner office was a rather large room, luxuriously furnished in starkly modern style. Nym walked across the softly carpeted floor and sat down on the long couch that ran the entire length of one wall. Unconsciously she smoothed the cushions beside her with a hand that seemed to tremble more and more.

When Lynn entered the room Nym greedily devoured the slender beauty with her eyes. Although she was twenty-three years old, Lynn seemed like a child, at once nubile and whitely tender.

5

Nym patted the couch at her side and Lynn came obediently and sat down, pad and pencil ready in her lap.

"I ... uh ... I want to ... to ..." Nym found to her horror that she was stammering like an idiot. With a violent effort she forced her voice under control. "I want to write a note to Mr. Samson—you know, the man who owns that property by Lake Okeechobee. I would like to—"

"Mr. O'Sullivan already wrote him last Thursday."

"Oh ... oh, I see. Well, in that case we can let it go. All right then, suppose we write to—" Suddenly she broke off. When she continued, her voice had a strangely pleading note in it. "What do you do for fun, Lynn?"

"I beg your pardon, Mrs. O'Sullivan?"

"I mean—I know it's a strange question, coming so suddenly—I just mean ... I simply happened to wonder about it, that's all."

"Wonder about what?" The girl's face was puzzled.

"Well, about what you do for fun. You know ... nights and all."

Lynn smiled. "Oh, I don't know. Go to the movies. Read. Things like that."

"Do you have a—a boy-friend?"

"Not really. I date now and then, but most of the boys around here are kind of dull, Mrs. O'Sullivan."

Nym smiled her famed, dazzling smile. "Isn't that the truth, though? It must be very difficult for a young, single girl away from home to find anything exciting to do here in Okeechee."

"You found something exciting to do, Mrs. O'Sullivan."

"I wasn't away from home, my dear."

"No, that's true."

Nym could not control herself any longer. She laid a hand on the girl's knee, knowing full well that its trembling was bound to be noticeable. "Lynn ..." she began hoarsely. The girl looked at her, fright growing in her eyes. "Lynn ..."

"Mrs. O'Sullivan, I think I'd better go watch the front office. Someone might want to come in."

"Don't go, Lynn. Please don't go." Great tears were beginning to roll down Nym's cheeks. Tears of excitement, tears of long pent-up tension, tears of self-pity. As great wracking sobs started from her throat she flung herself against the girl, her arms gripping her tightly as in a vise.

Lynn began to struggle. "Mrs. O'Sullivan! Mrs. O'Sullivan—please, what are you doing?" She fought strongly, straining to push Nym away and ward off the onslaught. But Nym clung tightly. With one hand she held the girl down and with the other she proceeded to unbutton the light summer dress. She threw all caution, all shame, to the winds and the short concise words of her desire gritted from between her teeth as she stripped the dress from Lynn.

The girl was silent now and fighting desperately to get away, but Nym was by far the stronger of the two.

"I'll scream, Mrs. O'Sullivan, I'll scream!" Lynn whispered, her terror-stricken voice strained by the effort of the struggle.

Nym did not care any longer. "Scream," she muttered between her clenched teeth. "Scream and let everybody come in here and find you like this. Go ahead, scream."

Lynn fell silent, saving her breath for the violent fight. She was wearing only a half-slip and it was jerked from her hips in one large motion. Nym cried out when she saw how beautiful the little white body was. Lynn was wearing the very smallest of pale blue panties that fit her slender, rounded hips as if they had been painted on. The matching brassiere clung closely to the hard breasts whose childishly pink points gleamed faintly through the net material.

Nym bent forward and placed her mouth upon the girl's. Lynn fought and strained, twisted and turned, but her mouth remained covered by the kiss which forced itself upon her. Nym's tongue gently caressed her gradually opening lips.

7

Lynn cried out against the constraining mouth and the seeking caresses. Then gradually the girl's struggles tapered off until she lay quite still with her eyes closed, allowing Nym's educated hands to do their work upon her.

Yes, the time came when she even helped, as Nym stripped the clothing from her own lush body, revealing blue-veined breasts that were so full they seemed swollen, their great dark eyes gleaming dully against the white flesh. And as Nym sank slowly beside her, Lynn started sobbing softly and her body arched in frantic ecstasy.

And then there were no sounds in the office but the sounds of love.

It had started a long time ago. So long ago that Nym could remember only a little of it, and that but vaguely. So long ago that it was in the root of things. That it was in itself the root.

Nym was supposed to have been a boy. Big Joe Bardolph wanted a son to take over the ranch when he himself would go to join his long-lost drinking companions around the eternal table, tilting their eternal steins.

But Nym was not a son. And Big Joe felt cheated. He felt cheated by his wife. It seemed to him as if she, night after night, had lured him into her bed, and in return for his bull-like strength and efficiency had treacherously given him only a puling girl-child.

"Sex," he roared. "Sex, that's all you can think about. And when the chips are down, what have you got to offer? Another female, that's what!"

Lucy stared at her husband with her great cow-like eyes, tears of self-pity flowing from them.

And Joe went on. "Well, I'll tell you what we'll do. There is a play by a clever, rowdy fellow named Shakespeare. It has a character in it that bears our name—Bardolph. Well, I'll tell you something. There's another character in it, a ruffian by the name of Nym. Very well, then. By all that's holy, our girl should have been a ruffian boy. We'll call her Nym."

After playing this joke on his infant daughter, Joe Bardolph proceeded to drink himself unconscious. And never again did he touch Nym's mother, who gradually declined into a bitter woman by virtue of neglect. It got to the point where Nym's mother hated the child. Every time she looked at it she was reminded of her failure to fulfill her husband's ardent wish. But it was a wish that, little by little, began to appear so unreasonable, so stupidly single-minded that she came to consider her husband a great hulking moron, and through him she saw the entire race of men as stupid morons. She decided never to have anything to do with men again.

Joe's drinking and Lucy's indifference soon put the ranch in the hands of the bank. Joe drew out his last hundred dollars, and full of whiskey and good cheer, drove his Model A truck smack dab into the side of the northbound express.

Then there were only Lucy and Nym, ensconced in a small, stuffy furnished room in Okeechee on the questionable borderline between Cane Hill and the more respectable section of town. They had nothing, and Lucy simply sat in a chair all day and stared out of the dusty window into the blinding sunshine. Nym played on the floor with a big cardboard box which had served as a packing-case for the few personal belongings which they still possessed when they moved.

It was thus that George Harvester found them when he came to offer Nym's mother a proposition. "Lucy," he cried in his boisterously jolly way. "How're you doin,' gal?"

Nym's mother hardly bothered to turn her head. "Go away," she said briefly and to the point.

"Now, Lucy, you know you didn't mean that!"

"If I didn't, I wouldn't have bothered to open my mouth, you fat-mouthed idiot!"

George laughed loudly. George always laughed loudly when he was insulted. That was how he had gotten to be chairman of the local political organization in power. That was how he had gotten to be alderman. That was how he had wormed his way into the country club, in spite of the fact that he was a tenant-farmer's son.

George patted Nym on the head. It was she who had opened the door at his knock. "That's a mighty nice little chicken you're sprouting here, Lucy." When Nym's mother did not answer he went on, "This ain't no place for her to grow up an' you know it. Right here on the edge of Cane Hill an' everything."

Lucy's face was set in bitter lines. "What do you suggest I do? Buy a mansion for myself out by the country club?"

"Well now, you could do worse, gal."

"I wish you'd stop calling me *gal*."

George Harvester became all business. He removed his big hand from Nym's head and she returned to her box on the floor. "Lucy, I've come to make you a proposition."

"I bet you have. You've had your eyes on me a long time. Don't think I haven't noticed. Only you were scared of Big Joe, weren't you?"

"Now, there ain't no call for you to talk like that. I want to give you a hand, Lucy, that's all I got in mind. Big Joe was always my friend and I just can't let his widow sit here in a little dingy hole on the edge of Cane Hill and starve to death."

"We're not starving."

George turned to Nym. "What did you have for lunch, kid?"

Nym stared at her mother wide-eyed, but no prompting was forthcoming from that corner, so she saw no way out of muttering the truth. "We don't eat any lunch. Mommy says we're dieting."

George's questioning was relentless. "You hungry, kid?"

Nym nodded mutely. She was always hungry.

Her mother started to cry. The usual big tears of sodden self-pity coursed down her cheeks in streaming rivulets. Nym thought how ugly her mother was when she was weeping.

Harvester went to the woman and put a big gentle hand on her shoulder. "Don't you cry now, gal. Look—elections are comin' up an' me an' the boys have got us an idea. We want you to run for county superintendent of schools."

The tears stopped as if a faucet had been turned off and Lucy raised her head in sharp surprise. "Superintendent of schools? Why?"

"You need a job, Lucy. A genteel job with a little dignity to it. It's the best we can do for you. For your own sake, for the kid's sake."

"But what on earth do I know about being superintendent of schools?"

"You was a schoolteacher when Joe married you, wasn't you?"

"Yes ..."

"You're bound to have had some ideas of your own about improvin' the schools you worked in, didn't you?"

"Well, yes ..."

"Okay. Here's your chance to try out a few of them."

"But why me? Why are you asking me? There must be a dozen people better qualified in Okeechee."

"Mebbe there is. But you're the only widow Joe left. Joe was a strong force in this community until he went and got himself killed! We think it would be a cinch to get you elected."

"But a woman? Wouldn't you rather have a man in a job like that?"

Yes. Why a woman? Lucy wondered after George had left.

It did not take her long to find out. A month after she had taken office, she and Nym had moved into a little cottage in the nice neighborhood just off the boulevard and Nym had started attending the grade school her mother supervised. Then one day George Harvester and a couple of the "boys" came calling on the new superintendent in her office.

"Hi there, gal! How you doin'? Real nice cozy little office you got yourself here. They treating you okay?"

There was a new primness in Lucy's voice, a new sense of self-respect, a modest searching for self-confidence and authority. "Hello, George ... gentlemen. Oh yes, everything is fine, thank you. What can I do for you?"

"Oh, nothin' much, Lucy. Just a little bit of a favor."

"Why, I'd be happy to, George. Seems like the least I can do."

"Oh now, you don't owe me nothin', gal. Hear tell they're fixing to build a new gym out at the Port Retreat school. That right?"

"That's right, George. Tell you the truth, I'm kind of excited about it. It's my first real chance to do some things about gyms that have needed doing for a long time."

"Bids all in?"

"Yes, the three that are required by law. And what's even better, the contractor they're going to award it to sees things my way, and for once we'll get some sun and air and enough plumbing and a decent floor in a gym."

"What's his bid, Lucy?"

"Now, George, you know I can't tell you that until he has been awarded the job."

"Lucy, you know damned well I'm not in the building business. You can tell me. I'm curious, that's all. An' don't worry about these gents. They're friends of mine."

Lucy looked from one to the other. "Well, seeing that it's you, George. But it mustn't go farther than this office."

"Don't worry, gal."

"Well, the bid is sixty-eight thousand dollars. And for that he will make an entire wall of glass looking out over the Gulf. Doesn't that sound wonderful?"

George looked doubtful. "Sounds like a lot of the taxpayers' dough."

"It's the lowest bid, George."

But it was not the lowest bid. The following day, by some miracle known only to George Harvester, a belated bid for sixty-seven thousand dollars was entered by one of the "gents" who had been present during the conversation. The bidding dateline was already passed, but the board felt that it could not afford to turn down so magnanimous an offer. And as long as the job had not actually been awarded to anyone yet, they were not breaking any agreements.

When Lucy tried to get her glass wall, her adequate plumbing, her decent hardwood floor, the contractor informed her regretfully that he was performing a public service by building the gym practically at cost and he simply could not afford to put in such unessential frills.

Eventually it appeared that he had not only skimped on the "frills," but on everything else. A whole generation of children grew up with splinters in their feet and knees from the poor-grade floor, with athlete's foot from the lack of adequate bathing facilities, with bad eyes from playing basketball by weak electric light in the middle of the sunny day. This might have gone on interminably if a section of the roof had not caved in a few years after the gym was built and the building had to be condemned and abandoned as being unsafe for occupancy.

But by that time the contractor was living in a very nice house which he had erected with the profits of his "public service."

The record does not show whether the fact that two children were killed and one maimed for life when the roof collapsed ever made any impression on this public-spirited citizen.

It made an impression on Lucy.

But by that time it was too late for her to do anything about it. For by that time she was completely and entirely in the claws of George Harvester and his political machine, which seemed to be operated almost exclusively by contractors and real-estate men. George himself never seemed to do a day's work, but then why should he? He was mighty useful to the vested interests.

And gradually those decent and kindly and honorable intentions which had been Lucy's when she had accepted the nomination disappeared and she did not even bemoan their loss. She simply ran for re-election every time it was necessary, and with the help of George and his friends she stayed in office till the day she died. A bitter woman. The ruined husk of a flower cast among thistles.

There were times during those long years while she continued in office and Nym served her time first in grade school and then in high when Lucy tried the golden anesthetic which had killed her husband. But the drinking spells did not last long. Lucy did not like the headaches and the nausea and the dreadful exhaustion that went with liquor.

There was another way that she found vastly more satisfactory. It grew out of hatred. Lucy loathed her daughter, who day by day was growing into a raving little beauty, trim of body, perfectly chiseled of face. By all rights, she told herself, the child should have been a son. If she *had* been, Lucy would not be at the mercy of a wicked world controlled by evil, greedy men. If Nym had been a son he could have supported his aging mother and she could have retired from the bloody battlefield and hidden in the parlor of some quiet little cottage provided by his loving, filial care. Somehow, it was Nym's fault that she was forced to be the pawn of George Harvester and his "boys."

Because Nym was not a son.

Nym never heard the last of it. Her mother harped on the subject day out and day in, at breakfast, lunch and dinner. At the same time she carried on a kind of continued lecture which expostulated on the subject of woman making her way in a man's world. There was only one way to do it and that was to become as hard and wicked as man himself. If there was one thing she was going to make sure of, she swore, it was that this daughter, who should have been a boy, was going to be as hard and self-reliant as if she were indeed a boy. Nym was going to be prepared to fend for herself, as her mother had never been prepared.

And the continued tirade on the subject of the wickedness and perfidy of men did a strange thing to the two women, shut up together as they were in the little cottage which formed the limits of their existence. They both became almost like men themselves—tough, unyielding, masculine in their thinking.

In school Nym had almost nothing in common with the other girls. Although she instinctively disliked boys and disturbed them, she hung out with them. Her greatest pleasure lay in outsmarting them and beating them in their own games. Beginning as the champion tree-climber of her class, she graduated into a top-notch pitcher, a fleet runner, an almost unbeatable basketball player, an ingenious builder of model airplanes. And many boys went home with black eyes and suffered the humiliating experience of having to inform their mothers that Nym Bardolph had licked them.

The full impact of what mystic forces were gradually released through the daily stream of vituperation that flowed from her mother became violently clear to Nym in her junior year in high school.

It was the night when Nym discovered that her mother, to all intents and purposes, had managed to turn herself into a man. That in self-defense she had actually entered the world of men and effaced her own woman-image completely.

It was the night when Nym too, to all intents and purposes, became a boy.

Her mother had company for dinner that night. The guest was a little red-headed teacher from one of the county schools. Lately Lucy had been favoring the little teacher. The girl seemed a good bet to become principal of the school in which she served, in spite of the fact that the school already had a principal.

The teacher was a soft-spoken, ingratiating creature with the strange sort of bland face whose expressionless doll-features you can never remember once they have passed out of your vision. She and Nym's mother seemed to have much they wanted to discuss, so right after dinner Nym retired to her room. After reading for a while she dropped off to sleep. It was a hot spring night and somewhere around midnight she awoke, her throat parched with thirst.

She got out of bed, her pajamas clinging to her perspiring body, and left the bedroom, heading for the kitchen. When she entered the darkened dining room on naked, silent feet she heard a strange groaning from the living room. Very quietly she approached the door and peeped in. The room was softly lighted by a single table lamp in a corner.

Lying on the couch, her face a mask of frantic ecstasy, was the red-haired schoolteacher. And bending over her, one knee resting on the floor, was Nym's mother.

They were both completely naked.

Deep-throated hoarse animal groans poured from the little redhead. Her eyes were tightly closed and her hands were clutched in Lucy's hair.

Nym stood like the salt statue of Lot's wife. She could no more have torn herself away from the spectacle than she could have stopped the heaving breaths that tore at her lungs as she watched her man-mother convulsively tormented by her love-drunk ecstatic escape. As the moans from the other room mounted into a frenetic, wracking sob, the furious pounding in her chest grew and grew until she had to cling to the wall for support.

She remained there for perhaps ten or fifteen minutes after it was all over and silence had settled over the house and the two women on the couch were asleep in their exhaustion, the smiles of happy little girls upon their faces.

Then finally she went shakily to the kitchen, got her drink of water, and returned to her bed.

But she did not sleep again that night.

And from that night on, Nym added a new field to her rivalry with the hated boys. She took their dates away from them. She was very clever at it. Very discreet. And many a little innocent girl, afraid of experiencing too close a contact with a boy, through Nym discovered hidden pleasures which she had never dreamed existed. Pleasures which she had never even imagined. Pleasures which could be indulged in without danger of unpleasant aftermath. Pleasures which could be freely enjoyed, for there is nothing unusual about a girl staying at another girl's house.

But while Nym was relishing these secret victories over the race of man, she was beginning to plan her big coup. That final devastating conquest which once and for all would satisfy her own and her mother's hatred and vindictiveness.

The great opportunity appeared during the summer after she graduated from high school. Nym was then eighteen years old. The opportunity's name was Sean.

CHAPTER TWO

It was almost noon when Nym Bardolph and Lynn emerged from the inner office.

The blonde girl was very pale and very quiet, but her great eyes betrayed a fulfillment and a peace that Nym had never seen in them before.

"You'd better go ahead and get some lunch, Lynn."

The girl stood quite still, staring at the floor. "Oh, Nym, Nym. I ... I couldn't eat."

Nym laughed. "Of course you can. Run along now and give it a try."

Lynn unlocked the front door reluctantly and left the office. Nym watched her trim figure as it emerged into the sunlight and disappeared slowly down the street. The girl seemed to be in a trance.

Nym sat down behind the big desk at which Sean had usually worked, receiving his customers and clients with a broad smile and a firm handclasp.

The interlude with Lynn hadn't done any good. It had not relieved the sucking hunger in her vitals. Neither had it been like old times. Nym regretted bitterly what she had done to the young girl. But she regretted even more what she had done to herself. Now that Sean was gone, she had thought she could once again "be herself" ... whatever that meant. But the experiment with Lynn—her reversion to earlier practices—had failed. She was no longer the bitter, hating, vindictive high-school girl of eight years ago. As the years had grown, so had she grown, and this first attempt in almost a decade to find solace in another of her own sex—to find relief, escape, oblivion—had backfired on her.

For she suddenly realized with sickening conviction that her use of Sean for the purpose of revenge on men had made the object of her abuse an object of love as well.

She missed Sean.

The man she thought she hated above all men, the man who had been a very symbol of the ruthlessness of men, the man who had *forced* her into marriage against her will, the man she had consequently destroyed.

This man she missed.

Was it abusing him she missed? Or was it the man himself?

She rose abruptly and went to the big safe that stood against the wall. With delicate fingers she twirled the familiar combination and swung the heavy door open. For an instant she searched, leafing through a pile of legal documents. Then she found the one she was after. She pulled it carefully free of the others and returned to her seat behind the desk.

For a long time she sat staring at it.

This was the final reason Sean had left—left her, left the business, left their home, left town.

This then was the ultimate instrument of her revenge. This paper, which represented an incomplete business transaction, was the club that she had used when she had administered the final blow.

It was a scene she would not soon forget.

"If you haven't got the guts, quit, Sean." She heard her own voice again. "I have done all your other dirty work for you for almost eight years now. I have every intention of completing this deal, if it's the last thing I do."

"But it won't do you any good, Nym, can't you see that? The street, the sewage line, the water main—all the expanded improvements will be fifty feet into the neighboring property. You couldn't touch it. It is the neighboring property that is worth money, not yours. And that property belongs to the city. They won't *have* to pay for a right-of-way."

"How many people know that?"

"You and I."

"So?"

"Well, heaven knows how many clerks in the office of the Register of Deeds during the last fifty years have been familiar with that particular deed."

"You know as well as I that when the question of the town expansion came up, *you* dug out that old deed. *You* brought it over here. It was covered with dust and almost rotted up with age. Nobody else has seen it. Only you and I—thanks to your impeccable political connections that make it possible for you to browse through the files of that incorruptible office."

"What good does it do you, Nym? The right-of-way is still on the city's property. That's the only thing you got out of our lifting that document—the knowedge that it doesn't do your cause a bit of good."

"I wouldn't be so sure of that."

"Look, Nym, within a very few days they're going to miss that deed. Let me take it back and let's forget all about it, huh? They're bound to have started looking for it already."

"We'll take it back when I get through with it."

"When you get through with it? What does that mean?"

She went to the safe and found the deed to their own property which bordered the old city property. She brought it back to the desk and laid the two documents side by side. "I'll tell you what I'm going to do." Her face was reflecting the pleasure she took in her own cunning. "I'm going to change the ownership of fifty feet of land. That's what."

She saw the shocked look come into his face.

"Nym, that's fraud." His voice was very quiet.

"It's smart business, that's what it is. That old deed to the city was made out fifty years ago. There isn't a soul that has looked at it for all that time.You said yourself that when the council decided to expand the city limits in that particular direction, knowing that the city owned some property out that way, there wasn't a single one of the council members who actually knew whether they were on city land or not. They only thought they were. The only reason they decided to go in that direction was because two of your buddies and fellow councilmen own property out that way, and you know it. They weren't even sure whether the old deed still existed. Well, it does, as you and I found out through a bit of honest thievery. Very well. When it is found, it is going to say that they guessed wrong by fifty feet and that the right-of-way must be purchased from us. And you and I are going to be very surprised, and of course very pleased that we can sell that precious right-of-way to the city."

"It's fraud, Nym. It's fraud and you know it."

"It's no more fraud than any number of private little deals and arrangements entered into every day of the year by you and by your fellow realtors and contractors."

"Not by me, Nym! I've never done a crooked thing in my life."

"No? How about when you wanted to marry me?"

"Nym, I have told you over and over and over that that was desperation. Darling, for heaven's sake, I wanted you so badly, I didn't care what I did."

"Yeah, I know."

"That's the only crooked thing I ever did, and that was in a good cause."

"Oh, come off it, Sean. This office owns property right now the acquisition of which involved the tears of old women and the cheating of defenseless children."

"That is *your* property, Nym."

"It is the property of the firm."

"You know as well as I that you are the firm, Nym. The properties that you refer to, you bought after you inveigled me into turning land and houses over to you."

"Inheritance tax, remember? You're a lot older than I, Sean."

"That's right. That is exactly why I started trading in your name. I did not do it so that you could gradually take over and put me out of business. Do you realize that today I own absolutely nothing in my own name? Everything—the business, the cars, the houses—everything is in your name."

"All right, all right. I know. Now how about this right-of-way?"

"No. I'll not be a party to it."

"If you're not, I'll never be able to get the old deed back into the registry files again. I don't have the freedom of that office like you do."

"Good. I'm glad to hear it. At least I seem to control that much of the business. The answer is still no."

"All right. I'll find some other way to do it."

He came to her then and sat down on the desk before her. He put his hands on her shoulders and forced her to look him in the eye. "Why do you hate me so, Nym? Haven't I always been good to you? Haven't I always loved you? Haven't I always adored the very ground you walk on? Why do you want to drag my name in the mud?"

"I don't use your name in my transactions. I've got a name of my own. A name my kind and loving father gave me. Nym Bardolph. Remember?"

"But Nym, Nym—you're still my wife."

"Am I? Good. Then how about this deal?"

"No!"

"All right then. As I said in the first place, if you haven't got the guts, quit. This is as good a time as any."

"Is that what you have been leading up to all these years?"

"Exactly."

"Do you want me to get out, Nym?"

"You might as well. It appears to me that you are of no further use to the business."

"And to you?"

Nym had gotten up from where she was sitting, confronting him. She replaced the two documents in the safe and started to leave the office.

"See you at dinner," she said and walked out into the street ...

That's how it had been.

Now Nym rose and, burrowing among the papers in the safe, she found the deed to her own property, eighteen acres of worthless orange groves—worthless until the recent decision on the part of the town council. She smoothed the document between her fingers and returned once more to her seat behind the desk.

But she could not concentrate on the matter at hand. Sean— and her final victory—kept crowding other thoughts from her mind.

He had been somber at dinner that night, a meal they had eaten in almost total silence.

Later on, after the newspaper had been read, with each apparently waiting for the other to speak first about the afternoon's argument in the office, Sean turned off the lights and checked the front and back doors as he always did. And silently, not having spoken, each went to a separate bedroom, a practice of many years.

When she was alone in her room Nym sat staring into the huge mirror over the dressing table. She saw a handsome patrician face surrounded by the soft and gentle curls of a modern haircut. She saw large, hazel eyes that now appeared to her sharp and hard. She saw fine round white shoulders, set off by the off-the-shoulder effect of her expensively styled peasant blouse.

But under the patina of studied smart elegance she saw no woman at all. She saw a man in woman's disguise. Or rather, she saw a kind of female Jekyll-Hyde who could bring her femininity into play when it might further her aims, or who could be as hard and self-reliant as a man when it suited her course of action.

She saw no softness, no yielding qualities, no dependence upon anything but her own cunning. A neuter creature of business, childless and lonely. A loveless monster of revenge.

And suddenly the thought of Sean's leaving became too much for her to bear. She had always hated him—so she thought. She had always worked for his destruction, patiently—like an ant carefully placing pine needle upon pine needle until a structure apparently far beyond the insect's strength and resources is completed.

But now the wonder she had worked to bring about had actually come to pass. And it gave her no pleasure ...

Seated at the desk, Nym snapped back to reality. She shook her head stubbornly to clear it of the unwanted thoughts, loathing the weakness that resided in her heart like an insidious disease.

Carefully and deliberately she smoothed the two documents side by side on the gleaming desk top. She examined them carefully. One, yellow with age, was covered with the fine penmanship of some long-dead county clerk or lawyer's scribe. She took a magnifying glass from the center drawer of the desk and examined the ink with minute care. It did not seem to have deteriorated appreciably.

She laid the glass beside the paper and, drawing closer a handsomely mounted memo pad, she reached with her other hand deep into the inner recesses of the center drawer again. Her hand came out holding a small bottle of black ink and a little envelope of pen-points. She dropped the pens out of the envelope, selected one with a fine point, and inserted it into a penholder. Then, dipping the pen in the ink, she slowly, painfully, attempted to copy the handwriting of the document upon the memo pad.

Her first attempt was very clumsy, the letters too big, the *m's* and *n's* pointed at the top rather than rounded. Before she tried again, she blew upon the writing until it was dry, then examined both the ink on the document and the ink on the memo pad through the magnifying glass. She hunched over her work, glaring through the glass, her eyes squinting. Finally she was satisfied. The difference between the two inks was so slight that she was convinced the change which she was planning would be unnoticeable to anyone except a chemist or an expert on old documents. She did not foresee any possibility that the change would ever be suspected or that the papers would ever be examined by detectives for any reason.

With a satisfied little shrug she gathered the papers and the implements together and carried them into the inner office. For the second time that day she locked the front door. She got the eraser fluid from Lynn's desk and brought it back with her. Then she closed the door to the inner office and set to work again.

Looking like an alert bird, her head tilted once more in an attitude of utter concentration, she carefully studied those sections of the yellowed document which she would have to change in conformity with her plan. The paper was extremely exacting as to the location of the city's plot of land. It became obvious that two sides of the lot would have to be shortened and the starting and finishing points of the measurements would have to be altered. She carefully considered the small spaces that would be left after the erasures and attempted to estimate the areas which she would need in order to rewrite the deed to suit her purposes.

Finally, using the ink eraser, touching the document delicately with the very tip of the little glass rod, she made the erasures she considered necessary.

She laid the paper aside to dry. Dipping her pen once more in the India ink, she practiced imitating the handwriting until her facsimile was almost perfect. Then slowly, letter by letter, she rewrote the deed, making the alterations.

Holding the document between thumb and forefinger, she waved it slowly and carefully in the air until the ink was dry. She laid it on the desk, ran the tip of her forefinger through the thin film of dust which had gathered on the desk top over the weekend, and very, very gently smeared a tiny bit of the dust over the spots which she had rewritten. She turned on the desk lamp and held the document close to the light. A slow smile spread over her face. With the naked eye it was impossible to detect the fraudulent passages.

Completely satisfied, she laid the deed aside. Her own deed was recent and typewritten. Using the eraser lightly and the same typewriter on which the document had originally been made, she made the changes necessary to conform with the altered city deed.

When she was through, she drew a deep sigh of satisfaction. She replaced the papers in the front-office safe and locked its door. Then she carefully put the eraser fluid in Lynn's desk drawer. The India ink, the pens and the penholder she carried out the back door and, making sure no one was watching, she disposed of the implements in one of the several garbage cans lined up in the alley.

Then she re-entered the office, locked the back door, turned out the desk light and went into the front office. She unlocked the street door and returned to the desk she had originally occupied.

Approximately an hour had passed since Lynn had left the office, and when the girl returned, it would appear obvious that Nym had simply held down the office while the girl was at lunch. In fact, it would appear that she had not even moved from her front-office desk. Fortunately no client had attempted to enter the office that morning.

Now, sitting behind the desk, Nym felt a flood of triumph surging through her. What she had set out to do had been accomplished and, at the expense of the men on the city council and the men who were her business rivals, she had arranged a little fraud that would set them all on their ears and—incidentally—make her a pretty penny.

The question of how she would get the falsified document back into the files of the office of the Register of Deeds entered her mind. And then quickly, as if her brain had shifted into another gear, the thought again slipped automatically to the man who, out of his slavish devotion to her, had stolen the document in the first place. Sean. Sean was no longer here to help her get it back. Now she would have to find someone else.

She wracked her brain, trying to think of a person who could and would help her, but as before, everything returned to Sean.

She was thoroughly annoyed with herself for letting Sean impose upon her peace of mind to such an extent. It was a development she had not counted on.

She thought with shame of the last night her husband had spent in their home.

Somehow, I must stop Sean from leaving, she had thought. Now when it was too late she had found that she needed him.

She had tried to shrug it off. As she sat staring at her own image in the big dresser mirror, she had told herself over and over, repeating it like a broken record, that what she needed him for was simply to get the document back to the file where it belonged before someone discovered that it was gone.

She told herself this over and over and over. But a strange and unrecognizable emotion kept interfering with her calculating train of thought. She wanted Sean to stay for an entirely different reason.

Is this love? she asked herself contemptuously. After all these years of careful planning and even more careful work, has my deliberate destruction of him ended up in love for him?

Whatever it was, she knew now that she must somehow make him stay. Make him *want* to stay.

At other times over the years when she had wanted something from him, when without his willing co-operation she could not continue her campaign against him, she had resorted to the method which she now decided to employ. It had worked before. Now it must work again.

Resolutely she rose from her seat before the mirror. She stepped to the middle of the floor, and admiring herself in the gleaming glass, she started to strip the clothes from her lush body.

She pulled the peasant blouse over her head, revealing a white satin strapless brassiere which confined her breasts. She undid the waistband of her full skirt and dropped it about her ankles. The white half-slip followed, and Nym Bardolph stood revealed in white transparent panties, generously garnished with lace about the thighs. She reached behind her back and released her breasts.

She faced the mirror complacently, her eyes resting approvingly on her own body. Her figure was slim, the hips almost boyish, but with a hint of curves that seemed to negate the very slimness which was the most striking thing about her lines. Nym's breasts were large, very large for a girl her size, but there was not a hint of sag about them. With a soft, sensuous movement, she lifted them gently with her hands, weighing them thoughtfully in her cupped palms. Finally the hands glided upward and over them, and with a sharp little intake of her breath she felt the wide peaks stir. When she removed her hands the points were taut.

Nym's fingers were trembling a little as they went to the waistband of her panties. She rolled the garment slowly down over her hips. It released itself reluctantly from her legs and dropped unnoticed to the floor. Unnoticed because Nym was admiring herself again in the mirror, her eyes roving over the dimpled flatness of her white stomach, over the mystic promises of shadowed recesses and nooks.

Finally she tore herself away from the glass and entered the bathroom adjoining her bedroom. She ran hot water in the tub, sprinkling a generous amount of bubble soap into it, and soon she was immersed in the soothing, fragrant liquid. Hurriedly now, she bathed, and after drying and powdering her trim, lovely body, she entered the bedroom. From the huge closet which formed one wall of the room she removed a black transparent negligee. She wrapped the diaphanous garment about her naked body and left the room.

As she walked softly down the hall she discovered a new excitement in herself. This was not like the other times when—for a similar reason—she had traversed the same distance. She knew that deeply within herself. There was another reason that palpitated excruciatingly in her vitals.

Outside the door to Sean's room she hesitated. She examined again her motives for this visit to a man whom she had never touched in love, but only in her attempts to gain advantages over him in their life-locked struggle which had lasted so many years. And she did not now understand herself.

Giving up, she gently eased the door ajar and slid inside. Sean's room was softly lighted by a shaded lamp on a bedside table. He was lying in bed, his arm locked behind his head upon the pillow, a cigarette drooping from the corner of his mouth. As Nym entered the room, he turned his head toward her inquiringly, but did not otherwise move.

"Sean?" She spoke his name hesitantly.

"Hmm?"

Nym was conscious of his eyes sliding over her thinly veiled figure. She knew that her white flesh shone luminously through the sheer material and the knowledge pleased her. "Sean … I …"

"Yes?"

She moved closer to him. "Are you sleepy, Sean?"

"Not particularly."

She sat down on the edge of the bed. "You want to make room for me?"

"No, Nym, I don't."

It was like a bucket of cold water over her shoulders, but she controlled herself. She slid the negligee from her shoulders and let it drop about her waist. As her full, proud breasts sprang into view, quivering with the motions of her arms, she watched his face and saw his eyes narrow. She saw the slight twitch of his hand on the cover, and she took it and put it against her flesh.

"Now?"

His hand was loose and open. It did not fondle her or make any motion at all. His face was expressionless and she felt a cold shiver run through her. Sean had never been devoid of reaction before.

"What do you want, Nym?"

"What?"

"You have never entered this room and offered yourself like this without expecting something in return."

"That's a cheap thing to say."

He removed his hand and reached for the light. "Let me sleep, Nym. I'm not in the mood for games. At any rate, I don't see that I have a single thing left that you might want to bargain for. So let me sleep."

She stayed his arm with a strong hand. "I don't want you to leave me, Sean."

"I know that."

"You know?"

"Certainly. When I leave, how are you going to get that deed back into the file in the Register's office?"

"That's not why."

"No?" He waited patiently, but now she could not try to explain what was in her. She was hardly aware herself that it was remorse, so how could she have told him? She sat there stupefied, unable to speak, her breasts gleaming in the lamplight.

"Don't cheapen yourself or your victory, Nym," he said drily.

"Don't... don't you want me?" She loathed the whine in her voice. She had not expected that she would want to crawl on this day of all days. It confused her dreadfully.

"I have never done anything but want you, Nym. Never. But it has been like loving a Siamese cat. When you pick it up to put it against your cheek to fondle it and show it your affection, it rewards you with its claws. It has been a hard lesson to learn. Yes, Nym, I want you. But I will not touch you."

There was nothing now for her to do but to rise and go. This she did, but when she reached the door, she stopped deliberately and made a last play for him by the process of putting her negligee back. She allowed him a full glimpse of her entire naked body, white and slender and curved and soft.

But when she raised her eyes she saw that he had put out his cigarette and was reaching for the switch on the bedside lamp. "I'll be leaving in the morning," he said.

She left the room, and as she closed the door behind her, she heard the click of the lamp as he put out the light to go to sleep. And that was how it had ended...

A shadow fell across Nym Bardolph's desk. She had been so absorbed in her own thoughts that she had not realized that anyone had entered the office. She raised her head and found herself looking straight into the broad, smiling face of an enormous man.

The man shook his head. "No, no, no, please don't get up, Mrs. O'Sullivan. Mind if I take a chair? I got an awful lot of bulk to hold up when I have to stand."

His laugh was an amazing thing to watch. It seemed to start at his feet and work its slow and ponderous way up his legs and through his broad trunk until it emerged like the roar of a wounded elephant from his tiny mouth. He shook, his chair shook, and the entire office reverberated and echoed with the raucous noise.

Finally he caught his breath. "Oh," he gasped, "I do get such a kick out of that. I been on one of those 'Fat Boy's' diets, you know. I should have a 'before' and 'after' set of pictures taken, I really should. Only there isn't any film big enough to get all of me on it."

He laughed again and Nym found herself wishing he would stop. She regarded his huge bulk as it settled itself wheezingly in a spindly, modernistic chair. The man seemed to be built in layers. Protruding over the edge of the seat were his voluminous thighs, and resting upon them was his barrage-balloon of a stomach. Arranged on top of the stomach was the chest of a rhinoceros, and perched upon this were some four to six chins. Hanging down on either side of the top two or three chins were the jowls of a bloodhound, and topping the entire layer cake arrangement was a shining bald dome. The man was all pink. In a manner of speaking it was a frightening pink, for it was not healthy. It was the kind of pink that formed a perfect frame for the small red-rosebud mouth that perforated the center of his foot-square face.

He leaned forward in his chair as far as his bulk would permit him and extended a hand so elephantine that Nym instinctively drew back from it. The man pretended that he had only meant to brush a little dust from the desk top. The smile never left his face.

"The man is Gordon," he sputtered. "Frederick Gordon, but most of my friends call me Tiny. You know how it is, the boys have gotta have their little joke."

Nym regained her equanimity. "Yes, Mr. Gordon. I'm very happy to meet you. What can I do for you?"

"Well now, Mrs. O'Sullivan. That kinda depends. Perhaps I can do more for you than you can do for me."

"Yes?"

"I kinda hate to bust right into business like this, Mrs. O'Sullivan. I like to get a little acquainted first. You don't know me and I don't know you … personally, that is."

"Personally?" Nym did not know what to make of the expression.

"Oh, I read the Okeechee *Record,* ma'am. Yes, ma'am, I sure do. Get lots of ideas from that nice little paper. I see your name in there and your picture too, every so often. Know you from that. You see?"

"Oh yes, of course. I see."

"But I don't know you to speak to. That's what I mean. An' you don't know me. Matter of fact, you couldn't be expected to know me. I live over on Cane Hill. Nice lady like you wouldn't be apt to know the likes of me. I own a couple of saloons over there. Trashy trade mostly. Drinks and a little gambling on the side."

"I see."

"Oh, don't bother to disapprove of me, lady. Ain't no harm in my establishments. No women. No fighting. I go to church pretty regular. I'm just a businessman like anybody else. Got a lot of friends over that way, though. Yes, ma'am, Mrs. O'Sullivan, I'm a happy man."

He fell silent and Nym wondered whether he was waiting for her to unburden her heart to him now that he had told her about himself. After a while she ventured, "Well, Mr. Gordon, it's nice to be happy. There are so few people who can claim that nowadays."

"Yes, ma'am. You're dead right. Danged if you ain't." Then he fell silent again. Expectantly silent.

She went on embarrassedly. "I...uh...I'm still wondering what I can do for you, Mr. Gordon."

The tremendous man looked out of the window. He spoke casually. "My lawyer tells me I've got too much loose cash lying around. He calls me up on the phone, danged if he doesn't, and says, 'Look, Tiny,' he says, 'I've just been looking over your assets an' you got too much loose cash around. Ought to tie some of it up an' make it work for you.' You see, I been doing pretty good with those saloons of mine an' the little bit of gambling. I'd kinda like to spread out a little. So I come to you."

"Why that's fine, Mr. Gordon. What kind of property might you be interested in?"

"Well, orange groves, for instance."

Suddenly, unaccountably, a cold shiver ran down Nym's straight spine. It was not what he had said that did it, nor was it his tone of voice. It seemed to be a mysterious premonition. But

Nym's voice was calm when she spoke. "You've come to the right place, sir. We have some very nice tracts up north a-ways in the central part of the state."

"I wasn't thinking of up north, ma'am. No, as a matter of fact I wasn't."

"Well, I'm afraid that's all I have in oranges. Perhaps we could work out something else. How about ranch land down around Okeechobee? It's some of the best grazing and vegetable land in the country. Ought to give you a good return on your money. You can easily run four cows to the acre down there without depleting the pasture."

"No …" he sounded hesitant.

"Well, did you have something particular in mind, Mr. Gordon?"

"For a fact I did, little lady." He turned his head now and grinned at her, and considering the repulsiveness of his fleshy countenance and tiny, round O of a mouth, his grin was surprisingly engaging. "I was kinda thinking of the eighteen acres of groves you-all own just north of town."

Nym felt the cold shiver again, more insistently this time. "But those groves are ancient, Mr. Gordon. They're overgrown with years of weeds and the trees are old and on their last legs. You wouldn't want them."

"I wasn't thinking of the oranges, ma'am. I'm not about to become a citrus grower."

"You're not?"

"No, ma'am. It's the land that interests me."

"But that land is useless, Mr. Gordon. It's inaccessible, far from any decent road. Why, it's a regular jungle up there."

Nym was keenly aware of the sharpness with which his little half-hidden eyes were regarding her. She began to tremble. She did not know whether it was with excitement or fear. "How did you know we have that land, Mr. Gordon? We have not advertised it for sale."

"Well, I've always thought I'd kinda like to have me a little of that land out that way, Mrs. O'Sullivan. So I went to the Register of Deeds. What's the trouble, ma'am?" he asked hurriedly as he saw her sway and turn pale. "You ain't feeling good? Can I get you a glass of water or something?"

"No! No ..." It was a weak gasp. Now she knew why she was trembling. And she also knew what Frederick Gordon wanted. "Please, go on."

"Like I was saying ... look, if you don't feel good I can come back some other time."

Nym made a weak negative gesture with her hand and he went on. "All right, just as you say. Anyway, I went to the Register of Deeds to find out what the story was out that way. I saw your deed to the eighteen acres. That's how I happen to know. I'd like to buy them eighteen acres, ma'am."

"They're not for sale, Mr. Gordon."

"Like I said, ma'am ... maybe I can do more for you than you can do for me I can take that useless jungle off your hands, Mrs. O'Sullivan."

Nym rose. "I'm sorry, Mr. Gordon. The land is not for sale."

"And I wouldn't dicker about the price."

"It's not a matter of money, Mr. Gordon."

"I'm real sorry you feel that way, ma'am."

Nym could restrain her curiosity no longer. Her voice almost betrayed her. "When did you go to the Register's office?"

It was quite a while before Gordon answered her. He had not taken his eyes off her face during this entire exchange. "A little while back, Mrs. O'Sullivan. I was real interested in that land. I still am."

"Why are you so interested?"

"I'm sentimental, ma'am. Like I said, I always wanted a chunk of that land up that way. I was born an' reared in a little cabin only a mile or so away from there. I always thought it was mighty pretty country."

"You seem very anxious about it."

"Oh now, I wouldn't say that. I'm interested in maybe trying to develop that region a little bit." He rose laboriously to his feet, his entire frame quivering and joggling with the movement. Nym thought she detected a thinly veiled threat in his voice as he continued, "In fact, I kinda went to a lot of trouble in the Deeds office. I checked and rechecked on all of that territory. It looks like it's got possibilities." He chuckled richly. "But maybe I shouldn't of said that to you. Now maybe you'll wanna do something yourself up that way."

"What made you come to me today, Mr. Gordon? Why did you not come to me a while back when you checked on this land?"

"To tell you the truth, little lady, I went back to that office today and this time your deed was missing. So I thought to myself, Mrs. O'Sullivan must be gettin' ready to sell that land. I better go and see her."

"Why me? Why not my husband?"

"Why, ma'am, that land is in your name."

"But this is my husband's business."

"I suppose so, in a manner of speaking. But I sort of understood that Mr. O'Sullivan left town today. On a sort of an extended vacation. So I thought you would probably be takin' over while he was gone."

So it was already known all over town? Nym shuddered inwardly. But her voice was quite steady now. "That's perfectly true, Mr. Gordon. But the deed is gone simply because I'm taking a little inventory of my holdings. I have no desire to sell that land."

Gordon sighed cavernously and went to the door. He put his hand on the knob, but before he opened the door to go out into the street, he turned. When he spoke, his voice was very, very soft. "Like I said, Mrs. O'Sullivan … I checked that land real carefully. When I went back today there was another deed missing. Now I wonder, ma'am, what can be the connection between the two? Why ain't neither of them there? I thought I ought to tell you, ma'am, that if I don't find out pretty soon, I'm going to have to have some of my boys look into the matter. I reckon they can find out for me, all right. They're mighty thorough boys."

Before Nym could answer he was gone and she watched him helplessly through the plate-glass window as he waddled down the street. He entered a big pale-green Cadillac which already was partly filled with men and was driven away.

Nym found that she was trembling violently. She rose from her seat behind the desk and, crossing the floor uncertainly, went to the large safe. She touched it lovingly, thinking of the two documents that lay immured inside.

How, she thought, how in the name of heaven am I going to get them back into the Register's files again without being noticed? Sean, Sean, why did I chase you away?

And in a shudder of sudden fear she saw her whole life clearly in a brief flash of self-recognition. It had all been spent in the setting of an elaborate trap. And now it looked as if the trap was about to snap shut on her.

CHAPTER THREE

When Lynn returned from lunch Nym hardly glanced at her, so occupied was she with her problems.

The girl stopped before the big desk and murmured, "I'm sorry I took so long. I ... I went home and took a bath."

Nym looked up sharply. "A bath? Did you feel unclean?"

"Oh, no. No, Nym. I ... I just wanted to look at myself."

Nym smiled slowly. She understood. The same thing had happened to her once, long ago. It had been the first time for her too. A wild, orgiastic night not long after she had seen her mother and the little red-haired schoolteacher together. The other girl had been a little brunette in whom Nym had discovered a pent-up emotional volcano that she had manipulated into furious eruption. The next morning, when she arrived home, she locked herself in the bathroom and languorously, sleepily, stripped her trim sixteen-year-old body. Then she carefully examined herself in the large mirror fastened to the inside of the door. No nook or cranny went uninspected. Her hungry eyes searched and searched. Finally she stretched herself in the warm, soothing water.

She had gone to sleep there and nearly drowned.

Now she asked Lynn the same question that had been on her own mind that morning ten years ago. "And have you changed any?"

The little blonde blushed. "Well ... no ... not really. Not anything you can see, anyway."

"I know. It doesn't show."

"Oh, Nym. I feel different, though."

"Bad?"

"No, no! I ... I feel ... oh, I don't know. Wonderful, I guess."

"Good."

"You ... you don't feel contempt for me now, do you, Nym?"

Nym laughed and rose from her chair. "You're a silly girl, Lynn." She came around the desk, and after glancing carefully to make sure that no one could see them from the street, she kissed the top of the girl's head. "Now, look. I'm going down to the courthouse for a little while. If anyone wants me, tell him I'll be back shortly."

She left the office and strolled slowly down the sunny brick-paved street toward the courthouse grounds. On her way she passed the Bijou Bar and Grill. She hesitated. Finally she shrugged and went inside. She found an empty booth and sat down. When the waiter came, she asked him for a Swiss cheese on rye and a Manhattan.

When he had gone to fetch her order, she propped her elbows on the table and rested her chin in her hands.

This was the same bar, the same table, the same time of day as when she had her first date with Sean O'Sullivan. It could not really be called a "date." It had been more like a command performance. Sean had been very forceful in those days. How well she remembered every moment ...

"I'll take a Coke."

"Don't you drink, Nym?" Sean said.

"Not when I can avoid it."

"Well, I won't force you."

"Not to drink, anyway."

"Look, Nym. I've got to make you understand me. The only reason I did what I did was simply because I just couldn't seem to get at you any other way."

Nym smiled bitterly, a surprisingly old smile for so young a girl. "*Get at me* seems an appropriate phrase."

He reached across the table and put his hand over hers. His voice was very gentle. "Will you marry me, Nym?"

It was a long time before she answered. When she did her voice was dry, dead. "It seems I've got no choice."

"Please. Please don't look at it that way. I couldn't help myself. I love you so much. Perhaps there's a little touch of insanity in me—in all men."

She did not answer him, but sat quietly, thinking of the scene she had had with her mother the night before.

High school had been over for a couple of days, and a graduated Nym had been wandering restlessly about the house, wondering what to do with herself, when her mother came in. She was terribly agitated. The minute she had the front door open, she started calling for Nym.

Lucy was wringing her hands, and great tears were rolling down her cheeks. She sat on the couch, twisting and turning as though she were in great pain. "Nym," she stuttered, "Nym … I don't know how to say this to you. Something terrible has come up."

"What is it, Mother?" Nym was completely calm. There were times when she was startled to rediscover that in many ways she was much older, much more mature, than her mother. "Now stop weeping and wringing your hands," she added impatiently, "and tell me what's the matter."

"There … there's a man who wants to marry you." It was a desperate cry.

Nym laughed out loud. Was that all? It had happened at least a dozen times before. Each time she had taken a certain joy in turning the suitor down as sharply as she could. "For goodness' sake, Mother. That's nothing to get upset about. It's happened before."

"But, dear, this time it's different."

"How is that?"

"The man threatened me. He threatened *us*."

"Oh, it can't be as bad as all that. Who is it?"

"Sean O'Sullivan. He's at least twenty years older than you and … and he's ruthless. Absolutely ruthless. He has made up his mind that you're going to marry him."

"Nobody can make me marry anybody, Mother."

"O'Sullivan can. Oh, If you only knew. If you only had the slightest inkling of what I have gone through this afternoon. He wants to see you tomorrow for lunch. He wants an answer."

Nym started toward the phone. "I can give him an answer right now without bothering to go and eat with him."

Lucy screamed and jumped to her feet. Her voice quivered and blubbered. "No, don't. Don't touch that phone! You just don't know. Oh, what I have been through today." She sank back onto the couch, weeping and tearing at her scarf.

Nym came back to stand directly over her mother. "All right. Now tell me what happened this afternoon."

Through her sobs and sniffles the story spilled out of Lucy. "Well … this afternoon about three o'clock he came into my office. Said he wanted to see me on important business and would I mind if he closed the outer door. He had a kind of wild look about him and I was a little afraid. You know how men are. You never—no, never—know what they are going to do. But he closed the door anyway and came and stood right in front of my desk. I asked him to sit down, but he said no thank you, he could talk better standing. And then it came out. He wanted you to marry him."

"Why didn't he come to me?"

"That was just it. He said he already had—three times."

"That's right."

"And you had turned him down flat. Or rather you wouldn't even have anything to do with him."

"Right, too."

"So he said he had no choice but to come to me."

"Why, Mother, that's the craziest thing I ever heard. What are we living in? The Middle Ages?"

"Oh, no. No, not at all. This is the Twentieth Century. Nobody but a modern man could have thought up the threat he presented us with."

"Threat?"

"Yes. Oh, dear, this is the most difficult part. Oh, I wish I didn't have to tell you, but I simply can't see anything else to do." Lucy jumped to her feet and started agitatedly pacing the room. "You see, it's about me. I ... well, we all commit our little indiscretions now and again ... and I've ... well, I mean ..."

"Has he got the goods on you, Mother?"

Lucy turned, startled. "The ... the what?"

"The goods. About your girl friends."

"Oh ... you ... you know?"

"For two years, Mother."

"I see." Lucy stood in the middle of the floor, her face pale and drawn, her eyes deep pools of torment. Finally she burst out, "Yes ... he ... he knows, just as you do."

"And he's blackmailing you? With me as the prize?"

"Yes, Nym. That's it exactly." Lucy began to weep again. "Oh, how could I ever do this to you? Why did I ever let myself get involved in such things?"

"Because of men, Mother. That's why."

"Yes, because of men."

"You loathe them and fear them and distrust them."

"That's right."

"I don't blame you, Mother. I'll go and see Mr. Sean O'Sullivan tomorrow for lunch."

"What ... what are you going to do?"

"I don't know yet. Let's wait and see. Good night, dear. And don't let it get you down. I'll figure some way out."

In bed that night Nym weighed all the possibilities. Her mother's living depended upon a political job. If Sean made good on his threat, Lucy would go hungry in her old age. Nym was not about to let that happen. She also sensed an opportunity through Sean to organize her life in such a way that, meeting men on their own level, she could gradually work her hatred, her vindictiveness, her fierce sense of competition with them, into the achievement of her ambitions.

Sean O'Sullivan was a very desirable catch in Okeechee. He had never been married before. He was rich. He was successful. The type of business he was in afforded her the very opportunity she was looking for. He was also a handsome, distinguished, personable man. If she had to get married she would as soon be tied to him as to anyone she knew.

She decided to accept his somewhat unusual "proposal."

At his office she raised her head and looked Sean straight in the eye.

"Yes, I will marry you, Mr. O'Sullivan."

"Sean, Nym, please—Sean."

"Sean. I will marry you. I do not pretend to approve of the manner in which you have forced me into it. Perhaps you think I should be flattered that you want me so badly that you are willing to stoop to coercion to get me. But believe me, I am not flattered."

His face lit up. "You will learn to forgive me, my sweet, believe me. When you become convinced of the sincerity of my love for you, you will forgive."

"I said I will marry you." Nym's voice was cold. "And I will, but only under certain conditions."

"What are they, Nym? Whatever you want, you can have, I promise you."

"I want to become a partner in your business."

"A partner?"

"That's right. I was not cut out to be a homebody. I prefer to function outside the home."

"Request granted. We'll get servants for the dirty work."

"And no children."

"Oh, now, Nym. You're not serious."

"I mean it. I would rather let you make good your filthy little threat against my mother than bear a child of yours."

"Do you loathe me that much, Nym? Please, Nym, forget the stupid, ugly threat I made. I swear to you I would never under any circumstances have carried it out."

Nym stared straight into his eyes. "Wouldn't you have? You're a man, aren't you? If you hadn't gotten what you wanted, and if you don't get it now, you would carry out your threat all right."

Sean's face showed how appalled he was at Nym's obvious distaste for him. "I swear, Nym."

"Spare your breath. No children."

"All right, Nym. If that's the way you want it, no children." Then he smiled confidently. "But you'll come around. The time will come when you will know me better ... maybe even learn to love me and want children yourself."

Nym ignored the hopeful enthusiasm in his tone. She went on relentlessly. "And instead of your making out a will, I want you to put things—material things—in my name. I want something out of this deal right away, instead of waiting to become your widow. I do not care to have everything taken away from me by taxes."

Sean gave up. "Very well. As you wish."

Two weeks later they were married. It was a lovely wedding. Lucy was appropriately teary and the bride looked lovely and virginal in white tulle.

That night, on their way north for an extended honeymoon, they stopped just south of the Georgia border in a luxurious motel. Sean engaged a suite, and after the bellboy had carried in their bags and had fetched ice and soda Nym's brand-new husband proposed a toast to their marriage.

"I don't care for a drink," she said curtly. She sat stiffly in a chair and watched him swill himself into a bacchanalian stupor, then. She saw the male cruelty rising in his eyes. She saw his hatred of her for what she was doing to him. She saw his determination to get his end of the bargain.

This will be my life from now on, she thought. Or at least until I get rid of him, after I am through with him. She made herself a promise that in all ways, within the limitations she had imposed, she would make him a good wife. She would be faithful to him. No more nocturnal expeditions to the homes of "girl friends." She would make his home presentable. She would be a good and useful hostess. She would present a satisfactory front for him so that he would not lose face in his community.

But underneath the surface she would burrow like a mole, digging her subterranean empire, tunnel by tunnel, until—honeycombed and riddled by her cunning—his rotten male world would collapse and sink into the earth to be buried there forever, and she would stand free, a monument to her revenge against men.

She did not flinch when he lurched from his chair and dragged her to her feet. Nor did she make a sound when his drunken fingers clawed at her going-away suit, ripping the material from her shoulders and hips until she stood before him in her brassiere and panties. She pressed her lips together when he fell upon his knees before her, his loose mouth slobbering words of frenzy.

She stepped back from him and deliberately finished undressing herself until she had completely denuded her youthful, lovely body. Then, determination in her eyes, she dragged him to his feet and led him to the bed. "Let's get this over with," she muttered between clenched teeth.

Then she made no movement, uttered no sound except for one sharp, animal cry of pain ...

Nym Bardolph ground her face into her palms, oblivious of her surroundings in the Bijou Bar. She pressed her fingertips against her temples, unaware that people who already knew that Sean had left her two days ago were watching her, some with pity, others with scorn, but all of them curious to know whether she had come to drown her sorrows.

She remembered only too well the years of their marriage. She felt again his early frenzy and her own sick feeling of revulsion when he came to her, demanding his end of the deal. She remembered the disgust with which she had listened to him when, having failed to arouse her again and again, he would crawl and plead and beg for her love, for just the tiniest spark of response on her part. She remembered now, with loathing for herself, how for a while she had gone through a phase where she had enjoyed arousing him, helping him remove his clothes and then letting her educated fingers and hands roam over his trembling body, their search and skillful stimulation growing gradually in intimacy, only to stop her little game short when his face contorted with the painful ecstasy of the ultimate moment. And she heard again his frustrated ravings that as the years wore on became whimpers and whines, until the day came when he no longer seemed to care. Then she knew that her torment of him would have to take another tack.

Lucy had died when Nym O'Sullivan was twenty-two years old. The woman had contracted a cold, it had turned into pneumonia, and the county superintendent of schools had slowly wheezed her life away.

This event coincided almost exactly with the days when Sean regained his manhood and once again won control over himself. He was then no longer the puling, begging, whining suppliant at her feet, but held himself aloof and refused to allow his starving body to be abused by Nym's perverse sadism.

The time had obviously come for Nym to change her tactics, and this she did with an alacrity that surprised even herself. She transferred her attentions from Sean's body to his business. If she could no longer emasculate him physically, she could emasculate him financially. His blackmail threat against her mother could never be invoked again, nor could he, except at peril to himself in the precarious community in which he functioned as a businessman, allow his marriage to appear a failure.

Nym had him where she wanted him. Little by little she asserted the business partnership and the financial settlement which she had extracted from him during that first interview in the Bijou Bar, and gradually she saw his holdings passing from his hands into hers.

It must have surprised him then to find her coming to his bed at night, willing, passionate, inventive, eager, fulfilling—no, going far beyond—his wildest dreams of blissful satiety in her arms. She came to him nude, her splendid body gleaming in the lamplight, her breasts quivering with the most apparent physical desire, her hands no longer cheating him, her mouth a moist cavern of accomplishment, her flesh a haven of blissful satisfaction. Or she came to him shrouded in a variety of veils of provocation which he, with eager, trembling hands, was privileged to strip her of—while she, with half-shut eyes, pretended to dream about and lovingly anticipate the final moment.

But every time this happened he paid a price. At first he did not notice this, so happily ecstatic was he in this new-found marital perfection. But after a while he did. And when the day finally came that he realized he must stop her, it was too late. While he had been under the anesthesia of her manipulations, Nym had graduated from being a novice at his trade to being his decided master and to being by far the more ruthless of the two. From deal to deal her ethics had deteriorated and her methods had grown shadier and shadier.

Sean was appalled, she knew. But still, as time went by, he could not deny himself the ecstasy of his inordinate passion for the beautiful and passionate woman she had succeeded in becoming.

Until last Thursday night, when he again had grown to become the master of his own flesh ...

And now, as she rubbed her fingers over what felt to them to be a mask of frightful evil, Nym Bardolph knew that Sean's victory over his flesh had been her defeat, and that Sean, through the rediscovery of his manhood, had turned her triumph into ashes.

Nym loathed herself, as womankind must loathe a hideous monster that devours its own spouse.

She raised her head suddenly from her hands and the waiter who had been standing silently by her side looked with startled eyes at her tortured face.

Nym picked up her sandwich and nibbled dispiritedly at it. She sipped the drink slowly. She glanced about the bar-room, noting but not really seeing the people who sat about looking, as do all Florida people, as if they had not a thing in the world to do except enjoy themselves. While her eyes roamed restlessly about, her mind shook off its dull and painful lethargy and once again applied itself to the task at hand. How was she going to get the two documents back into the files in the office of the Register of Deeds without the help of Sean? And once she got them back, how was she going to call the attention of the city council to the fact that she "owned" the land which they were planning on using? She could not very well go directly to them herself since no one was supposed to know about the pending plans as yet. Everyone on the council took it for granted that the strip of land belonged to the city. Had they not taken this for granted they would have searched the title more thoroughly. But they had not. The tradition had been that the tract of land north of the city belonged in its entirety to Okeechee. They had had no reason to question this tradition.

And now they had gone ahead and planned their whole expansion program, their new housing program, complete with playgrounds, parks, churches and shopping district, on the presumption that they were entirely on their own land.

This whole new section of town, which was to be the modernistic pride of Okeechee and which was to stand as an eternal monument to the civic-mindedness, the progressiveness, and the resourcefulness of the present city council, could not exist without the right-of-way to permit the city to lay water mains, sewers, cables, and the main boulevard which was to skirt the elongated residential district.

The exact location of this planned right-of-way, which for geographic reasons could not be placed anywhere else, now "belonged" to Nym Bardolph.

It was important that this fact be discovered by someone on the inside. Nym could not go to the city officers herself and point it out. Someone in the know would have to stumble over the disconcerting truth of the deeds and call to the attention of the council the fact that their negligence in not checking the city's deed was going to mean that they would either have to buy fifty feet of land from Nym Bardolph—and Nym would set her own price, you could be sure of that—or else abandon the whole program which had been in the making for nearly a year.

All right, then. Nym needed three things. First of all, she must get the documents back into the files where they belonged. Secondly, she must see to it that the council's plans were prematurely revealed to the press and public, so that it would become a matter of loss of face for the council if they should be tempted to back down on their plans. Third, she must find someone on the inside who would be her accomplice to the extent of "discovering" the "truth" about the deeds.

The apparent hopelessness of the tasks before her frightened Nym. She wished she had never started any of it. She wished Sean were back. She found herself wondering where Sean was, what he was doing. She was about to rise and leave the restaurant when she saw the young man come in. Instantly, as in a flash, she sensed a possible solution to all three of her problems and sank back into her seat, her face composing itself into an inviting smile.

It was young Johnny Martel who had entered the restaurant. He looked around the room and when he saw Nym and had absorbed the obvious invitation in her smile, his face lit up and he started toward her.

During the thirty seconds it took Johnny to cross the floor to her booth, Nym relived certain brief interludes from her eventful life which suddenly took on remarkable importance. Interludes that concerned Johnny Martel...

The children formed a tight circle around the combatants who had been rolling on the sandy ground. Now both were on their feet, warily circling each other.

Twelve-year-old Nym, her jeans raggedly torn down the side of one leg, her T-shirt hanging in tatters from one shoulder almost exposing what was still only a bud, shook the sand from her hair and rubbed her eyes briefly to clear them of the dirt. All about her she heard the shrill voices that egged her and Johnny on. The childish spectators seemed to be split into two camps, boys in one, girls in the other. In the voices of the boys she detected raucous derision. In the girls' shrill cries she heard naked, undisguised hatred.

The girls for Johnny, the boys for her. It was always that way, for Nym was more a boy than a girl. The boys knew it, so did the girls, and they took their sides accordingly.

There seemed to be a red haze over Nym's eyes. She tossed her head in irritation to clear it away, then lashed out wildly with her right and caught Johnny Martel in the pit of the stomach. She saw his eyes glaze, but he stayed gamely on his feet. The heart had gone out of him, though. And Nym saw the big tears of frustration beginning to trickle down his freckled cheeks. She swung hard against his chin and saw his head jerk back and felt the moisture of his tears on her knuckles. She hit him again and suddenly she realized that he was not hitting back, that actually he had hardly hit her at all during the entire fight.

She remembered now the soft, open blows that he had struck, the futile way in which he had clawed at her clothes when they were rolling on the ground, the pleading look in his face when she had provoked the fight to prove herself his equal.

He won't fight me, she thought bitterly, because I'm a girl.

With all her strength she struck him again in the face and saw him fall. Then she was standing over him. "Get up you," she gritted furiously. "Get up and fight like a man!"

But he stayed down. He lay flat on his back, his big brown, cowlike eyes staring straight up into her face, his cheeks wet with tears.

She turned on her heel, and forcing her way through the admiring crowd, she walked away, kicking her toes in the dirt, beating her clenched fists against her thighs, her insides taut as a bowstring...

Fifteen-year-old Nym ran swiftly through the vacant lot, jumped lithely over the fence and wove her way, running at full tilt, through the palmettos and scrub brush of the flats beyond the town.

She heard Johnny behind her, gasping for breath, desperately trying to keep up with her fleet-footed flight.

It amused her, the pursuit, the chase, and she chuckled to herself as she ran. Suddenly she flung out her arms and threw herself to the ground on a poverty-stricken little patch of sunburnt grass. She lay there hugging herself ecstatically and laughing and rolling back and forth when Johnny, heaving for air, dropped at her side.

When he had caught his breath she propped herself on one elbow and looked down into his sweat-stained face. She let her eyes roam over his lanky, skinny, adolescent frame.

"You wanna wrestle?" She laughed.

Johnny Martel grinned weakly. "You'd beat me."

"Dam right I would. Good thing you know it, so you won't make any mistakes."

"What kind of mistakes?"

Then she was suddenly silent. For once she had nothing to say. She had not meant to invite the innuendo. She did not like to be reminded that she was a girl.

She lay down on her back and closed her eyes. "Shut up," she said, "I wanna listen."

"Listen? To what? There isn't anything to hear."

"Oh, yes, there is. The silence. Hear it?"

Johnny listened dutifully. "It just sounds like nothin' to me."

"Ain't that a fact," she muttered ungrammatically. Then, just as abruptly as she had become quiet, she lurched into active speech again. She sat up and hooked her arms around her pulled-up knees. "Whatchu wanna do when you grow up?" That sounded stupid to her from her grown-up pinnacle of fifteen years, so she amended the statement. "I mean when you get through school."

Johnny thought long and hard. After due consideration, he made a profound pronouncement. "Loaf," he said with finality.

She stared at him in consternation. "Loaf?"

"That's right."

"For Pete's sake! Why?"

"Going to school is hard work. I need a rest."

"For the rest of your life?"

"Yeah. What's wrong with that?"

"Haven't you got any ambition?"

"Aw! Ambition. All you really need in this wicked world is something to eat and a roof over your head and plenty of time for fishin'."

"Well, if you aren't the laziest thing I ever heard of!"

"Naw. I'm not lazy. I'm going to work real hard at fishin'."

She laughed, and then her face grew dreamy and serene. What she said made her expression utterly incongruous. "I'm going to put every man in town out of business when I get out of school."

Johnny turned his head where it was lying in the grass and stared at her. Then, thinking she was joking, he laughed.

She turned on him furiously. "You don't think I can do it?"

He was quite calm about it. "Maybe you can and maybe you can't. All I know is that you're just talking through your hat."

She got to her feet with a jerk. "Wait and see," she said angrily.

He rose too. "What would you want to do that for, even if you could?"

"I can and I will."

"Okay, so you can. What do you want to do it for?"

She started to move away from him then. "Because I hate men!"

He followed her and caught her from behind by the arm. "Me too?" he asked quietly.

She jerked to get loose. "All of you."

Then she felt his arms move about her and suddenly his hands were cupping her young breasts and she was pressed against the entire length of his body.

"Please don't hate me, Nym," he whispered softly against her hair. "Because I'm going to marry you when we get out of school."

She fought to get away from him, but he held her fast and she was deeply disturbed at the strange, sucking sensation that seemed to squeeze her stomach and then let go and then squeeze it again. "What for?" she gritted between her clenched teeth. "So I can go fishin' with you?"

"Worse things could happen."

"Not me!" she cried. "Not me, never!" Then she gave a desperate lurch and managed to lunge free of his encircling arms. "Let go of me, you fool," she gasped, and sped away back toward town.

After a while she grew aware that he was not following her. She slowed down to a walk.

And then she realized that she was shaking all over ...

The eighteen-year-old bride walked down the aisle on the arm of her husband. Nym's eyes defiantly swept the crowd. And through the filtering haze that nervousness had laid over them, those eyes picked out familiar faces here and there. Boys she had fought, girls she had known during the last two years. Girls she had known too well. Mothers, fathers, all the people who make up communities and form the amorphous mass that one may either hate or love, according to one's temperament and station.

Nym had nothing but contempt for them. For Nym was on her way. Her hand was firmly hooked around the strong left arm of the man who was to be her stepping stone, her ladder, and the scarlet carpet she would walk to glory on. Nym knew where she was going.

The last face she saw just before she left the church was the sun-tanned, outdoor face of a lowly typist in a county office. A typist who as a part-time employee had plenty of time for fishing.

Johnny Martel was weeping. Great tears were running down his face. He made no attempt to hide them.

Nym hardly noticed him ...

Now as Johnny Martel approached her table, his face lighted by boyish pleasure, Nym reflected that his easygoing personality had given him a kind of life and a kind of peace which she, with all her driving ambition, her bitterness and vengefulness, would never attain. He was not rich, nor was he what you might call a prominent citizen, but his honesty, his kind smile, his lack of assertiveness had won him a position of trust in the community.

Johnny was young. Yet he already was secretary to the Register of Deeds. And he was the junior member of the City Council.

Johnny Martel, then, was the obvious answer to her problems.

Nym reached out her hand toward the approaching man. He took it without saying a word and she pulled him to a seat opposite her.

Johnny looked at her for a long time before he found his voice. "I'm sorry, Nym. I heard about Sean's leaving just a little while ago. It seems like a dirty thing for him to walk out on you like that."

Nym smiled crookedly. "Perhaps I should have gone fishing with you in the first place, Johnny." She noticed with satisfaction the light that appeared in his eyes.

He has not forgotten, she thought. He has been eating his heart out for me during all these years. Well, Johnny, you're about to get your chance.

She finished her drink, carefully giving the appearance that she was very thirsty for it. Then she raised her eyes to his. "Buy me another, Johnny?" she asked.

He regarded her worriedly. "You think you ought to?"

She almost laughed in his face. Men were easy to trick. They were like little boys, all their self-conscious nobility lying below the surface, ready to be exploited by any clever woman. Ah, weak female, how lucky you are to be in the hands of the noble, protective male, she mocked silently.

"I kind of need it, Johnny," she murmured in a very small voice.

"Okay. One more. Then I think you ought to quit. This is not the way to fight your problems."

"You're so right, Johnny." There was more meaning in the brief statement than Johnny Martel could possibly understand.

When the drink arrived at the table, Nym picked it up with trembling fingers and stared into its depths, tears welling into her eyes. She felt her other hand suddenly covered by one of Johnny's.

"Oh, Johnny, Johnny," she muttered brokenly. She took a long sip, closing her eyes painfully during the action. It was an almost perfect performance and Martel was falling for it like a ton of bricks. Almost any man would have, she knew, for she was a beautiful woman, and all her life, even when she was gay and carefree, men who did not know her as did Sean, had felt a powerful upsurge of their protective instincts when they regarded her. Somehow, she always managed to look frail and appealing.

Johnny said quietly, "Look, Nym, I know you've never given a damn about me…"

She looked up quickly. "Oh, that's not true, Johnny. That's not true at all. I…I never quite trusted myself with you." She noted his quick intake of breath and was satisfied.

"I…I mean…" he continued hesitantly, "maybe this is a dirty thing to do, coming out with something like this so quickly on the heels of your separation, but…but if there's anything I can do…" He ground to a halt helplessly.

Nym managed a dazzling smile through her tears. "You don't know what that means to me. You just don't know."

"Well, I mean…I'd do anything for you, Nym."

"Would you, Johnny? Really?"

"Anything, Nym. Anything. I…I've always felt like that."

"I think I know, Johnny. I think I've always felt it, too."

"Ever since we were kids together."

"I knew then, dear. You remember our fight? Remember how you wouldn't fight back?"

"I couldn't fight you, Nym. I just couldn't."

"The boys called you a coward."

"I didn't care."

"You were always so good. Remember when you asked me to marry you after we graduated?"

"How could I forget?"

"We were so young then, Johnny." Nym sighed deeply. "If we had known then what we know today, things might be different."

Johnny smiled a little tremulously, and Nym inwardly gloated. Like a little boy, she thought. He's soft like a little boy.

He said quietly, "If we *had* known, you might have been a great fisherwoman today, Nym."

In her mind's eye she saw herself, sunburned, peaked cap perched on the back of her head, motor-greasy jeans covering her legs, her rough, coarse hands clinging lovingly to a big smelly fish, a look of moronic triumph on her face. The human race conquers the untamed beast!

She quickly buried her nose in her drink. "That's right," she murmured insinuatingly.

He took her hand again and spoke quickly. "Look, Nym. I can guess what it must be like to wander around today, kind of lost. I...I was figuring on going out to the beach this afternoon. I've got a new boat, you know. It's a regular little cruiser. Sleeps two." Suddenly he stopped, embarrassed, afraid that she might have misunderstood him. "I mean..."

She raised her face to his. "Yes?"

"I mean ... would you like to go along? And ... you know ... get your mind off your troubles? You might enjoy it and perhaps you could forget for a little while."

How melodramatic he sounds, she thought. But she looked straight into his eyes. "Why, thank you, Johnny," she said. "I'd love to go."

CHAPTER FOUR

M r. Frederick Gordon, known among his friends as "Tiny" and among those who feared and hated him as "that louse," waddled into his little cubicle of an office at the back of the Sand Bar, his largest and most prosperous saloon.

He dropped his vast hulk in a creaking swivel chair that violently protested the assault of his weight. For a long while he sat staring out of the dirty window that opened out on a court-yard glaring in the brilliant Florida sunlight. His "boys"—three in all—who had followed him into the small room, ranged themselves along the wall and waited patiently for their boss to speak.

Gordon finally turned in the chair and faced the room and his henchmen. When he spoke, his voice was soft and puzzled. "Something mighty funny goin' on, boys. I can't quite figger out what it is. But I mean to find out. Jock"—a small dried-up shell of a man nodded briefly—"you sure you double-checked in them files?"

"Yeah, Tiny. Neither of the deeds is there."

Jock had been a lawyer, and not a bad one, before he had been tempted to fool with some securities belonging to a client of his. He had been out of the pen for only six months and was quite grateful to Gordon for giving him a job. He felt he owed a lot to the fat boss.

Jock continued, "You looked yourself, Tiny."

"I know, I know. An' if neither of us could find them, they simply ain't there."

"That's right." Jock tried to look modest, but did not succeed very well.

Gordon pursed his little rosebud mouth. "Okay, then. That dame is working up some kind of a deal. Damned if I can guess what it is, but I sure can smell a rat. An' I'll tell you boys something. I want that land of hers. I got no idea whether she realizes what the City Council is up to. Maybe she's just doin' exactly what she said—takin' inventory of her holdings. Maybe she ain't. I wanna find out. An' I got a real hunch that the answer to the question has something to do with the disappearance of that city deed. Two bits them deeds, wherever they are, are keeping each other company. So here's what I want you to do. Looie—tonight I want you to pay a little visit to that gal's office an' see what you can find in the safe. That clear?"

Looie, a lanky reprobate with a pimply face, said, "Okay," and dropped his head as if he were retreating into deep thought.

"After you get them documents we'll have a look at 'em and then we'll go on from there. Somehow we gotta make her sell me that land. We can't just steal a deed and appropriate the land, that's a cinch. But maybe them documents will give us a clue as to how we can get at her. If she won't sell peaceful-like, mebbe we'll have to persuade her a little. You got that, boy?"

They all nodded and Gordon swiveled his chair around and returned to his contemplation of the sun-blanched courtyard.

Tiny began to chew his fingernails. He never allowed himself this luxury in front of his men because he was ashamed of the habit. He thought it made him look like an overgrown baby, which it did. Now he chewed contentedly on the little flakes of horn and thought of the lucrative deal that lay ahead.

That was the way it had to be. The best deals always lay ahead. No matter how many lucrative machinations he had pulled off in the past, Tiny was never one to rest on his laurels. There was no sense crowing over something once it was won—the joy was in the winning, in the thrill of the conquest.

But he remembered them. As surely as if they were listed in a carefully tended scrapbook, every conquest had its rightful place in his memory. Every businessman he had ever bankrupted, every piece of property he had ever grabbed, every rich bitch who had ever whined for a little more time to pay her gambling debts.

Tiny remembered them all.

But when he added them together, the credit side of his ledger did not balance the debit. No lucrative deal, no thousand lucrative deals, could wipe out the stain. It dated back a long, long time—back to a time better forgotten—but it was still there, just as painful as the day when it happened...

Tiny Gordon had never expected to be asked to join the Tigers. He was fat and ugly and unpopular, and the Tigers was the smoothest club in the high school. And it came as quite a shock when Dick Crane, football captain and president of the Tigers, approached him one spring afternoon.

"Hi, Tiny." Even in those teen-age days, no one ever called him Frederick or Fred. Fatso, maybe, and sometimes Tubby, but never anything that did not label him as an overweight slob.

"Hi, Dick. What's up?"

"Well, uh, the Tigers might be having a little picnic out at Willett's Woods this Saturday. Care to come along?"

Tiny was flabbergasted. Would a fish swim? "Dick, don't you fellows in the Tigers like to be kind of private? After all, I'm not a member."

"Well, you see, that's all part of it. Your name has, uh, come up a few times and—"

"Me? To join the Tigers? You're kidding."

"Now hold on, Tiny, I didn't say that. We were just discussing it, that was all, and then we got the idea maybe you'd spend the day with us and the fellows could kind of look you over, know what I mean?"

"Oh, sure. Trial period, huh?"

"That's it. Only it won't be easy."

"Huh? What do you mean?"

Dick Crane looked at him seriously. "Well, you know the Tigers, Tiny. They're a pretty tough bunch of guys and you'll have to go some to keep up with them."

"Oh. Oh, sure."

"Especially with the girls."

"Oh. Yeah, I see what you mean. Well, just tell the fellows I'll do my best." It was spoken with light-hearted bravado, but underneath the surface there was a note of quiet desperation. For above all things, Tiny Gordon feared girls and their constant mockery of him. Not that he did not desire them—oh, no, at this adolescent age he was wracked by lust for the dainty creatures. But who among the girls of the high school deigned even to recognize him as a possible partner? Who would even walk down the street with such a ton of blubber?

But now it would be different. He was going to be a Tiger, and that changed everything. The Tigers were the greatest—and the whole school knew it. No girl would turn down a Tiger.

Tiny got little sleep until Saturday. He was going to a Tiger picnic and for the first time in his unhappy existence he was somebody. It was too exciting; it kept him awake nights even more than the strange visions of feminine flesh that had troubled his nocturnal rest for the past few years.

On the fateful day, Dick Crane got things rolling. Hot dogs and three-legged races were okay for the other outfits, but not the Tigers. A jug of moonshine, pure and powerful "white lightning," took the place of hot dogs and Cokes. And other pastimes, requiring less equipment and organization, substituted for three-legged races. As the sun sank slowly behind the luxuriant Florida foliage, Dick took Tiny aside.

"Okay," he said. "The boys want to make sure you can do everything a real Tiger can. Are you game?"

"Game for anything," Tiny said. But he wished he were as bold and fearless as he sounded.

"Good boy. Tell me, what do you think of Matilda?"

"Matilda? Not bad, not bad." Despite his forced nonchalance, Tiny would have gladly given an arm and a leg to get next to Matilda Cabaniss. Pretty, and developed beyond her years, Matilda was a sought-after queen, partly because of her beauty, but mostly because of her extreme selectivity in the bestowal of this selfsame beauty. Every guy in school knew it was hard to get a date with her, but that did not stop them all from trying. It was hard—but certainly worth the effort. It was rumored that she went "all the way"—but only for Tigers.

Tiny knew Matilda Cabaniss well. He had not said ten words to her in all his young life, but he knew her well. A high-school boy can become very friendly with the girls who dominate his dreams. And on many a hot summer night Tiny Gordon had crawled up the walls of his stifling bedroom with the mental image of Matilda as the object of his unfulfilled quest.

And now the fantasy was about to become reality. "Dick, do you think it'll be okay? With Matilda, I mean ... "

"Tiny, wake up. You're a Tiger now. Well, almost, anyway—and you know Matilda would never turn down a Tiger, don't you?"

Of course. He should have known better than to mention it. But it was so hard to grasp this wonderful new fact of life. It was hard to understand that these were the Tigers and he—Fred Gordon, once nothing but a despised fat slob—was now one of them. Well, almost one of them.

Matilda proved willing enough. She took his hand and led him away from the others, finding a small clearing in the woodland that seemed ideally suited for its use as a bower of romance. The leafy trees hung low over them and the grass was soft and springy. And best of all, the voracious Florida ants were all busy on other projects. Tiny's dream was about to come true.

They sat down in their snug shelter and he fumbled for words. "Uh, what do you say, Matilda, want to talk a while first?"

She shrugged. "What for? It's dark enough. Or at least it will be in another few minutes."

Tiny shivered. "Listen," he said, procrastinating, not feeling at all like a real Tiger, "listen to the crickets."

"Crickets?" Matilda smiled archly. "Those aren't crickets, those are zippers. You think we're the only ones off by ourselves like this?"

"Oh..."

"Well, what are you waiting for?" With coquettish fingers she dallied with his shirt, at last opening it. "Bashful?"

"Who, me? Naw..."

"Well, then."

Tiny took the hint. Slowly he began to draw off the shirt.

"Wait," Matilda said. "Maybe I'm the one who's bashful. Tell you what—you stay here and get all ready for me, know what I mean? And I'll go behind the bushes for a minute and get ready for you."

A perfect solution as far as Tiny was concerned. Matilda disappeared in the surrounding underbrush, and he started undressing feverishly. With the girl of his dreams out of range he felt no embarrassment, only haste.

"Almost ready, Tiny?" The invisible Matilda seemed to be as impatient as he was.

"Almost."

"Please hurry."

"Okay, I'm doing the best I can." A knotted shoelace was holding him up, and he was far too excited to make his fumbling fingers act with any degree of dexterity. But like a young Alexander cutting the Gordian knot, Tiny solved the problem with a sharp yank. The lace broke, but the shoe was off—and in seconds, so was everything else. "Ready now," he called.

The hidden voice tinkled in a kittenish giggle. "All right. Lie down on the grass and wait for me. I'm going to give you a nice surprise."

"Okay."

"And close your eyes."

Tiny closed his eyes and lay stretched upon the grass in the warm twilight. It was a supreme moment, one that he wanted to etch forever in his book of memories. The dream-girl was no longer a dream and the school pariah was no longer a social outcast. The world was good—Tiny Gordon was about to become a Tiger.

"Here I come …" The sweet voice sounded closer.

"Hurry up," he wheezed.

"And here's your surprise."

A raucous many-throated warwhoop struck his ears and he snapped his eyes open. From out of the surrounding bushes the Tigers advanced, all ten of them, each one gingerly balancing an upside-down pie of cow dung in his hand.

And with the beautiful—and of course, still fully clothed—Matilda Cabaniss directing them like the coxwain of a crew, the Tigers gave Tiny his surprise.

Cringing on the turf, his naked and misshapen body pelted and befouled, Frederick Gordon passed from boyhood to manhood. To the Tigers it was a prank, a big joke that would be good for laughs for weeks to come. But to their victim it was a moment of pain that would last a lifetime. Never again did Tiny Gordon trust anyone; never again did he allow himself to be duped by a living soul. The battle was on, the battle between the world and Tiny Gordon, and only when one or the other had conquered would it cease.

And now, with the business deal to end all business deals in the immediate future, the world would soon recognize who was the conqueror and who the conquered.

Tiny Gordon loved lucrative deals. And the tougher they were to pull off, the better he liked them. He thought with contempt of the people in the nice end of town and contemplated with pleasure the day when he, Frederick Gordon of Cane Hill, would be able to dictate whether or not those same nice people would be allowed to have their fancy new city development. He would like that. No, he would love it. It would be better than having a woman. For a brief moment his mind clouded with the old familiar despair. It had come hard to Tiny Gordon, the discovery that no woman, decent or indecent, could love or want such an elephantine mound of flesh as he.

But then his face cleared again and he dwelt lovingly on the pleasure it would give him to be able to dictate his terms to those sanctimonious, self-righteous so-an'-so's on the other side of the dividing line between Cane Hill and the better part of town.

After a while Tiny Gordon began to smile.

The trim little boat rocked gently in the swell of the tidal waters around the mouth of the river. The anchor rope was taut as a violin string and wavelets slapped the hull softly in the brisk breeze.

In spite of her expressed contempt for fishing, Nym was lying stretched out on the forward deck enjoying herself. There was peace out here on the water, and the expanse of the horizon around them seemed to stretch and stretch the distance between her and her problems until the latter seemed almost to disappear.

She opened her eyes and looked at Johnny. He was not fishing very enthusiastically. Now and again, with a desultory swing of arm and wrist, he would deftly cast, then slowly and with little skillful jerks reel in, only to repeat the entire procedure. But Johnny's heart was obviously not in it.

Nym closed her eyes again, pleasantly aware of the fact that his glance was on her more often than on his lure. And rightly so.

She had dressed carefully for the occasion. A white nylon blouse with short sleeves and tied in a knot about her waist was stretched and strained by the taut push of her full breasts. Her hips were sheathed in tight black shorts, and a goodly expanse of olive skin showed between the blouse and the waistline. She had tied a white scarf around her hair to hold the unruly curls in place.

She had been lying flat on her back, but now she lifted one knee, knowing full well that from where Johnny was standing in the stem, what with the brevity of her shorts and the fullness of their legs, he would be able to see the bottom edge of her white nylon panties.

She opened her eyes briefly again and noted with satisfaction the stunned look in his face as he stared at her furtively out of the corner of his eye. But he made no move toward her. He flung his spinner with a vicious toss and reeled it in with unaccustomed speed.

"You want a beer, Nym?" he asked, and she could sense the strain in his voice.

"No thanks, Johnny." After a moment she continued, "We should have done this a long time ago."

"Yeah."

"Things might have been different if we had."

"You don't care much for fishing, though, do you?"

"I like it out here. Fishing hasn't got anything to do with it. It is so peaceful."

"Makes you think, doesn't it?"

"Sure does." She rose from where she was lying and perched herself on top of the little cabin so that she was sitting right above where he was standing. "You're a good fisherman, Johnny."

"How do you know? I haven't caught anything yet."

She smiled coyly. "You've caught me."

"Have I?" He looked up at her and there was pain in his eyes.

Suddenly she hated what she was doing to this nice young man who had never harmed her in his life. At least, had never meant to.

"Well, I'm here, aren't I?"

"Yes, I guess you are."

Then there was a long silence and finally she asked softly, "What are you thinking about, Johnny?"

He did not look at her. "I was thinking that it's too late."

She was curious. "What's too late?"

"You and me."

Then there was another long silence. "Why, Johnny?"

"I'm engaged to be married, Nym."

She almost laughed, partly at the idea that this unambitious young man was about to take unto himself a wife, and partly because of the tension that was rapidly growing between them.

After a while he continued, all the while throwing his silly lure and reeling it back in, as if the action had some deep significance of its own. "We're figuring on doing it next month."

"Why, that's wonderful, Johnny."

He looked at her now. "So I got no business being out here with you."

"Well, why not, for goodness' sake? We're not doing any harm."

He looked steadily into her eyes. "You know how I feel about you. How I have always felt about you."

She looked away, out over the water, the brilliant sunlight blinding her as it was reflected in jewel-like perfection from the waves and ripples. Ruthless as she was, she did not like herself very much at that moment. "Who's the lucky girl?"

He answered curtly. "You don't know her."

"I'd like to."

"No, you wouldn't."

"How long have you been engaged, Johnny?"

"A year."

"Well, for heaven's sake, why haven't you married her yet?"

"You need money to get married."

"You expecting some money next month?"

"Just a little raise. We've finally given up trying to figure some way for a lazy bum like me to make a killing. We're going to take a chance on the little raise."

Nym saw another bait which she could use now. She was pleased to know that this might be easier than she had expected. "Maybe I can help you, Johnny."

He looked at her and his voice was dry. "Why should you?"

"Maybe because I like you."

"I wish you'd told me that eight years ago. It's too late now."

She was amazed at the strength of the bitterness in his voice. She realized only too clearly what he must have gone through when he had seen her walking down the aisle with Sean.

She jumped from the roof of the cabin down into the stem of the boat. She stood by his side for an instant, then said, "Excuse me a minute, Johnny." She went into the cabin and closed the door.

Inside, she sat on one of the bunks and stared at the bulkhead opposite her. She sat like that for quite a while, making up her mind. There was a great hesitation in her now that she had gotten to know Johnny a little better.

But then her hardness asserted itself, and the intensity of her own need to carry through what she had started. Johnny wanted two things. He wanted her, even if he had promised to marry another, and he wanted money.

Well, he could have both.

She untied the knot at her waist and shrugged out of the white silk shirt. She reached behind her back and unhooked her brassiere. After removing it from her shoulders, she dropped it on the bunk beside her. Then she put the shirt back on. Before fastening it in front she cupped her straining breasts with her hands and kneaded them thoughtfully. She weighed them and let them drop and felt the elastic give of her skin as it took their full weight.

After a little while she retied the knot at her waist. She did not button the shirt and it formed a deep V that reached from her throat to the bottom of her ribcage, revealing her gleaming olive skin. Then she rose and looked at herself in the little rectangular mirror that hung over one of the bunks. Her action had had the desired effect. The promising peaks of her bosom showed through the thin material. She nodded her head and turned toward the door.

She was breathing unnaturally fast as she left the cabin and joined Johnny in the stem of the boat. He turned to greet her and she saw his eyes widen as they came to rest on the front of her shirt. She heard the deep intake of his breath and noted the quick, futile movement of his hand on the gunwale.

She stepped close to him, but he drew away and she did not pursue her purpose at the moment. She climbed again to the top of the cabin and sat there, her legs dangling. "I'll take that beer now, Johnny."

He fumbled in the icebox, punched a can open and brought it to her, his eyes never leaving the front of her shirt. When he was close to her, she reached out and ruffled his short reddish-blond hair with her fingers.

"I wish I *had* told you eight years ago, Johnny," she whispered.

He turned away without answering and returned to his rod. But he did not pick it up. He sat down on the gunwale and stared into the rippling water. "It's too late now, Nym," he muttered.

"Is it?" Her voice was bright.

"You're married and I'm about to be married."

"I'm separated and you're not married yet. That's not quite the same thing."

He did not answer that, but from the expression on his face, she could tell that he was turning the thought over in his mind.

Boldly she said, "Johnny, look at me." As he turned reluctantly, she threw her shoulders back. She knew that he could see right through the shirt. "Am I still desirable?"

"Oh, Nym!" It was a choked moan and he looked as if he were about to cry.

She laughed then and raised her beer can. "Here's to you and me, Johnny." She tilted the can to her lips, then stood up and stretched luxuriously. "I'm going swimming. How about you?"

He did not answer, but turned and stared at her in bewilderment.

Nym kicked the sandals from her feet, then very deliberately she undid the catch at the side of her shorts. Looking Johnny straight in the eye, she dropped the small black garment. It fell about her ankles and she stepped free. Now, for all the coverage her shirt and transparent panties gave her, she might as well have been naked.

Johnny took a step toward her, but controlled himself, his eyes sweeping over her half-veiled body and his sun-tanned face slowly contorting into a mask of raging desire.

Beautiful and dark she stood before him, then she untied the knot in her shirt and shrugged out of it, deliberately letting her breasts dance with the movement. She saw that Johnny had begun to tremble. She turned her back on him and felt his eyes on her rounded hips where they gleamed through the panties. She walked to the bow of the boat and then turned toward him, her fingers at the waistband of the panties.

"All the way, Johnny," she cried gaily and slid the garment down along her legs and off. She straightened up and let him have a good look.

Then suddenly she plunged into the water.

Nym swam quickly away from the boat toward a sandbar that protruded above the surface some two hundred yards away. The cool water felt soothing and wonderfully relaxing as it flowed along her naked body. She rolled over once or twice, the skin of her breasts, taut with the cold, gleaming momentarily in the foam that surrounded her. During one of her turns, she saw Johnny's body, divested of surplus clothing, describe a swift arc through the air from the top of the cabin. He hit the water with hardly a splash, and she turned and began to swim in earnest.

As the sandbar drew nearer and nearer, she heard the laboring, swishing sound of Johnny as he began to gain on her.

The chase was fraught with excitement and she redoubled her efforts. When she felt the sand under her feet, she plunged forward toward the little island. When the water came to her knees, she started running, laughing and remembering the other time Johnny had chased her. When the water was only up to her ankles he caught her and flung himself at her. Together they went down and rolled over and over, their splashing bodies in the cool water.

Then Johnny had a tight grip upon her and she lay panting, her bosom rising and falling with the effort to regain her breath, the gleaming water rolling from her in jewel-like droplets. Johnny looked down at her, his eyes wild and his face contorted with desire. Nym found that she was surprisingly pleased by the feel of his tense body as it lay close to her.

Then he flung himself against her and his lips found her breasts, and when his hand touched her she cried out and arched her body frantically out of the water. Then she sought him herself and found him and suddenly the world seemed to be obliterated in seething foam and the love of a man—who for the first time in her life gave Nym complete fulfillment.

Later they swam lazily back to the boat and climbed aboard. They did not put their clothes back on, but dried themselves and opened more beer. Entering the little cabin, Nym stretched out on one of the bunks and Johnny sat on its edge, his eyes caressing her glorious body.

She ran her hand across his chest. "Come and stay with me tonight, Johnny," she whispered.

"I—I can't, Nym. We shouldn't have done this." "Oh, Nym, it was heaven—but we shouldn't have done it."

Her hand followed its relentless course and she saw his mouth begin to twitch. "Tonight?" she repeated.

He fell upon his knees beside the bunk and started to caress her with his mouth. His lips slid over her breasts, teasing them into taut attention, and soon their breaths were labored again and his mouth wended its maddening way along her flesh, leaving kisses in its wake. Then she tensed furiously and her hands, white-knuckled, caught the edges of the bunk and little sobbing moans sounded from deep in her throat.

Suddenly she caught him by the hair and bent his head back until the tendons in his neck stood out like knotted ropes. "Tonight," she gritted. *"Tonight!"*

When she let go, he fell forward, his face buried in her breasts. "I love you, I've always loved you, I love you I love you I love you," he babbled.

Her purpose accomplished, she smiled.

Nym Bardolph pulled up the big Cadillac in front of her house. She sat for a minute in the soothing silence of the tropical night and reviewed the day's happenings. Then, smiling to herself, satisfied with all that had occurred, she eased her lovely body out of the seat and slammed the door behind her. She entered the house, humming softly, and went into the living room and turned on the lights.

A small figure rose from the couch facing the big picture-window. "I ... I'm sorry if I startled you," said Lynn. "The terrace door was open and I just came in to wait for you."

Nym stared at her in bewilderment. "What are you doing here?"

Lynn's voice was petulant. "Where have you been all afternoon?"

"Why ... out with ... why, it's none of your concern, Lynn."

"It is my concern, now. You were out with Johnny Martel, weren't you? In his boat?"

"What if I was?" Nym strolled nonchalantly to the coffee table and helped herself to a cigarette. "That doesn't give you the right to barge in here like this."

Big tears began to form in Lynn's eyes. "You—you don't mean that, Nym."

"Of course I mean it."

"But what about this morning? Didn't that signify anything?"

Nym laughed and threw herself on the couch. "You silly little goose, of course it did. But look, after all, I didn't *marry* you."

Lynn sat dejectedly. "You just don't know what I have been through. When you didn't come back after lunch I closed up the office..."

Nym sat up abruptly. "You what?"

"I closed up the office."

"You had no right to do that."

"I was going crazy, Nym. Simply crazy. I didn't know where you were. I searched up and down the streets for you. I came out here in a taxi and the maid told me you had driven to the beach with Johnny Martel. I—I didn't know what to think!" The little blonde began to cry.

Nym grew angry. She rose and wandered nervously around the floor. "There's no call for you to think anything."

"Don't I mean anything to you?"

"Naturally you do."

"And wasn't that why you wanted me this morning?"

"Yes, Lynn. It was. But it does not mean that I'm going to give you an accounting for every step I take. Is that clear?"

Lynn rose slowly. "You don't feel anything for me at all, do you?"

Nym's bubble of anger finally burst. "Oh, get out of here, you sniveling little brat!" She turned away furiously, and behind her back she heard the little gasp of pain and the running feet and the quick slam of the outer door.

Then, suddenly, Nym forced herself to think more clearly. She could not afford to make an enemy of Lynn just now. No telling what the girl might be capable of doing if she got upset enough.

Nym ran out of the room and out into the front yard. She looked around, but there was no sign of Lynn. She jumped into the big car and, kicking it savagely into life, she roared down the driveway and swung out into the boulevard. She turned toward town.

She had only gone a few hundred feet when she caught up with Lynn running along the sidewalk as fast as she could. Nym drew up a little ahead of her and jumped out of the car.

Lynn tried to avoid her, but Nym caught her and held her fast, her arms tight around the sobbing little blonde. "Lynn," she murmured into the golden hair, "Lynn, Lynn, Lynn. Don't be so upset, please. Please! I was just a little out of sorts. I took it out on you. I didn't mean to. Please forgive me. Come. Come on." She led the girl to the car and helped her in. Then, getting in herself, she swung the big machine around in a wide U-turn and headed back to the house.

When she pulled up in the yard, she came around again, helped Lynn out, and took her inside. She placed the now docile girl in a chair. "I'll get us a drink," she murmured and went to the little bar against the wall. As she was fixing the drinks she heard Lynn behind her.

"I'm so miserable, Nym. So frantic."

"This morning you were happy."

"But I thought you loved me then."

"Now don't you start that again, you hear?"

"I mean it, Nym. If … if I was sure you didn't love me now, after … after … well, after this morning, I don't know what I'd do. I'd … I might even kill you!"

Nym laughed and returned to the girl with two shots of neat whiskey. "Here, drink up. It'll calm the killer instinct in you."

They both lifted glasses and gulped the burning liquid. Nym put out both hands and ruffled the blonde hair of the girl gently. "You mustn't get so upset about this, Lynn."

The girl's fingers came out and curled about Nym's rounded nude thighs below the black shorts.

Nym felt the pointed nails digging into her skin. A shudder ran through her.

Lynn's voice was choked as she spoke softly and intensely. "I'll never let you go now, Nym. Never!" She dropped to her knees and pressed her face against Nym's flesh.

Nym tried to pull back. She thought of Johnny, who might arrive at any time. He must not find her like this. "Not now, Lynn," she breathed. "Not now. You must go."

"No, no, no, no, no, no ..." The girl sounded hysterical.

And then Nym felt the other's fingers tugging. Before she could do anything about it, something like an electric shock went through her. For a brief moment she tried to remain upright, but then her knees gave way under her and she crumpled to the floor.

Now she no longer cared. Nym writhed under the ministrations of the little blonde girl to whom she herself had taught the art that very morning.

Later that night, much later, Nym left Johnny sleeping and went down into the living room of her home. She walked slowly to the bar and poured herself a drink.

She was nude, and as she sat on one of the barstools she regarded herself in the huge mirror that adorned the wall over the fireplace at the end of the room. She was a not unpleasing spectacle and—somewhat tiredly—she smiled at her own image.

Little girl, you've had a busy day.

The thought of Sean went through her mind briefly. But so much had happened and the conquest of Johnny had changed matters to such a degree that right at the moment she was not feeling any great need for Sean.

Her eyes swept the room and came to rest on a wisp of pale blue nylon that lay on the carpet. It was almost hidden under the couch. She jumped from the stool and walked across the floor. She was rather pleased with herself when she thought of the dispatch with which she had managed to get rid of Lynn after the episode on the floor.

She had driven the girl home hastily, but not so hastily as to arouse Lynn's suspicions. On the way back, Nym had stopped at the office. A strange feeling of unease had been disturbing her. But after the nocturnal visit to her place of business she had felt better. And when she'd returned to her home, she had found Johnny sitting dejectedly on the front steps, waiting for her.

Now she picked up the little garment and held it in front of her. Suddenly she laughed out loud.

What a day it had been! Easy pickings.

For someone else it had been quite a night.

Promptly at midnight, Looie entered the realty office by the back door. It took this talented craftsman only one minute to open the door and five minutes more to open the safe. It took him an hour to look through every document. It took him another five minutes to relieve himself by cursing when he discovered that the papers he was seeking were not there.

Meticulously he put everything back in its right place, closed the safe again and let himself out into the alley, relocking the door behind him.

Mr. Tiny Gordon, owner and operator of the Sand Bar and other lucrative enterprises, swore wildly when Looie returned to him with his tale of failure.

He called Jock into his presence, and after the sulphur fumes had cleared and Jock understood what the problem was—to wit: the documents were at present unobtainable—this gentleman suggested most sensibly, "Look, Tiny, those documents are bound to turn up. If they are not in the safe down there, Mrs. O'Sullivan is no doubt through with them and they will show up in the Register's office. Don't get so worked up about it. In a few days, when it won't look so obvious that I'm interested, I'll check once more. They'll be there then. Have a drink, Tiny, and relax. They aren't going to lay those streets and sewers and things tomorrow. Relax."

All Jock got for his troubles was another stream of vituperation. "That slut is up to something. What the hell is she doing with them documents? I wanna know!" Tiny's voice climbed to a thin scream. "If she's fooled around with them things, she'll get it. You hear? She'll get the full treatment!"

Jock tried to be reasonable. "How would you know if she's fooled around with them, eh, Tiny? You haven't ever seen either one or the other of those deeds. Admit it, old man, you don't know what's in them."

"Listen, you slimy little shyster…" The fat man saw Jock's eyes become small, like the heads of pins, and he saw the greenish tinge that settled over the lawyer's face. Instantly he was contrite, for he and Jock were friends, and friends were a rare commodity in Tiny's life. "Aw, Jock, don't take me seriously. I'm all fouled up. There was nothing personal in it. It's that dame. I been watching her. She ain't above a little fraud. Even if she is, that's not the question. Her husband is—or was, whichever it might be—a member of the council that decided on this expansion deal. You can bet your bottom dollar he knew what he was doing when he voted for it. Or maybe she was the one that told him how to vote. She's been doing a hell of a lot more of the buyin' an' sellin' during the last few years than he has. I'm telling you she knows something about that land up there that the council don't. And I wanna find out what it is. I got a sneakin' suspicion it ain't gonna come as a surprise to me. 'Cause I'm pretty damned sure that she owns—somehow or other, maybe honestly, maybe not—the land that'll make the difference when the chips are down. An' I'll tell you something else—she's gonna sell me that land, if I have to beat it out of her britches. That clear?"

Jock's voice was dry. "It's clear, all right. But I'll tell you something, Tiny, just between you and me. The days of land-grabbing are gone. You can't just stake a claim in this part of Florida any more. If you're going to get that land, it will have to look—on the surface, mind you—like a fair and square deal."

"It'll look like a fair an' square deal, don't you worry about that." Tiny's voice was very small and very tight. It seemed strange for such a voice to come out of such a hulk of a body. "When I get through with her, she'll be begging me to buy that chunk of real estate." He nodded his head curtly, and Jock faded from the room.

Tiny rose from his swivel chair when he was alone. He went to the sink that perched on the wall of his little office and ran himself a glass of water. After a brief mouthful he spat it out.

Damned Florida water! Tasted like chalk! He pressed a bell on the desk and a waiter came running.

"Ginger ale. Bring me some ginger ale."

When he had it, Tiny Gordon settled back in his chair, savoring the tart flavor, his eyes staring unseeingly at the wall. If I can't have it myself, he thought, I'll see to it that the piece is spoiled. I'll see to that all right!

He tried to think of money, great heaps of it. He tried to think of power, bucketfuls of power. He tried to think of dictating to the august, honored, respected City Council. But none of it pleased him.

What Tiny Gordon really wanted was a woman.

CHAPTER FIVE

The soft, yielding little redhead stared at Johnny in utter bewilderment. "What are you talking about, Johnny? You're babbling like a fool!"

Johnny Martel could not look at his fiancée. Although he had known her for a number of years now—and known her intimately for a year—she seemed to be a stranger to him suddenly. "Mickey," he stammered hesitantly, "I don't know how to explain this to you, but something really good has come up. Something good for both of us," he added hastily. "I'm about to quit my job at the Register's office and I'm about to make some real money. Doesn't that sound good?"

"You're going to quit your job?"

"That's right. Nym O'Sullivan has asked me to go in with her."

"You mean in real estate?"

"Yes."

"Why, that's wonderful, Johnny. Just wonderful. When do you start?"

"Any day now."

"It seems to me you have earned a kiss, darling." She rose from the couch where she had been sitting and crossed the room toward him.

Johnny watched her lush curves with sudden distaste. It puzzled him fiercely—this strange and unwonted dislike of her.

Mickey Stanton noted the look in his face. She stopped just before reaching him and said quietly, "What's the matter, Johnny?"

He looked away from her. "Nothing."

"You look funny."

"I guess I'm just excited."

She came to him then and plunked herself on his lap and put her mouth against his. Her little pointed tongue parted his lips and caressed them enticingly. After a while she began to squirm ever so slightly and her breath came more rapidly. Her sharp nails scratched at the back of his neck and finally she took one of his hands and placed it against her breast.

Johnny felt the familiar full firmness without experiencing any reaction at all. His hand rested inactively against the breast.

"Don't you want to, Johnny?" she whispered against his mouth.

"Not right now, Mickey."

He could feel her lips forming a smile, and she murmured, "You're getting old."

"Maybe I am," he said curtly and rose and walked away from her.

With a sick, sinking feeling inside him, Johnny Martel thought back to the old dreams about a carefree life devoted chiefly to fishing. It had not quite worked out as he had planned it. Somehow Nym's marriage to Sean O'Sullivan had made a drastic change in Johnny's life. His spirit and his zest, his laughing good-nature, seemed to have wilted and drooped and died. Although no definite spoken promises had ever been made between him and Nym he had always thought of her as the girl he wanted to marry. Her sudden arrangement with O'Sullivan had come as a complete surprise to him. But Johnny had managed to hide his suffering rather well.

And as the years had passed, he had deliberately dismissed her from his mind and substituted in her place the warmth and rich femininity of red-headed Mickey Stanton. Gradually, as he had grown into manhood and maturity, he had grown too in a desire for responsibility. His sole purpose in life was no longer fishing, although he was still an avid devotee of the sport.

But now, he thought, everything is ripped open again and Nym is dangling under my nose, and here—in the face of Mickey—I am ridden by my guilt.

He turned toward the girl. "Mickey," he began, "I ..." But he could not say it. He went to her, and forced himself to kiss her long and hard. And after a while he made the love to her that she demanded.

As he tried to lose himself in her soft, enveloping breasts, he thought of Nym ...

Two days later, having done what Nym had asked of him, Johnny gave notice of his resignation from the job he held in the Register's office. The office staff was sorry to see him go, for Johnny had been a pleasant working companion. He was told that if he ever needed it, his old job would always be there waiting for him. Knowing what he now knew, Johnny could feel his face turn scarlet with shame at the kindness which was being showered upon him so liberally.

That same afternoon, the story of the City Council's expansion plans was somehow leaked to the Okeechee *Record*. It was banner headline news the following morning and a mad scramble for lots in the area north of the city began. Nym's office was swamped with requests, but she turned them all down.

Johnny, in spite of the fact that for another month he was still an employee of the city, got into the habit of dropping by Nym's office every afternoon in order to learn the ropes. He found that as long as he was with her he was gay and happy and carefree, but the minute he left her presence he would think about the forged documents, now resting in their regular places in the file cases from which they had originally been removed. His dreadful feeling of guilt would then settle over his mind like a fog, his stomach would churn and his heart would beat faster in a pumping, driving rhythm of fear.

Johnny had never done a dishonest thing before in his life and what he had now done out of desperate love was costing him much, to say the least.

It was a new Johnny Martel that walked the streets of Okeechee, and people began to notice the change. The more they remarked about it, the more frantically Johnny tried to gloss over his terror and his ugly conscience. The more he fought against his guilt, the sicker he got inside.

Mickey Stanton grew more and more confused as the days went by. Eventually the time came when she began to wonder whether she had really ever known Johnny. She began to doubt very strongly whether she wanted to marry this man who moped and sulked and snapped at her on the slightest provocation. She became increasingly aware of the talk that was going the rounds of the town, ugly talk about her fiancé and Nym Bardolph. But somehow she could not bring herself to confront him with what she had heard. For a while she bided her time, and it was perhaps well that she did. For that was how she came to meet Sean O'Sullivan.

In the middle of the afternoon just two weeks after Johnny had returned the forged documents to the files in the Register's office, he dropped in as usual on Nym. Lynn was out of the office on an errand and Nym took him affectionately by the hand and pulled him into the inner office. She closed the door and waved him to a chair.

"Sit down, Johnny. I want to talk to you."

Johnny, his whole being glowing in her presence, sat obediently, all fears, all guilt forgotten for the moment. "Yes, darling?"

"It's only a couple of weeks more before you move in here for good. Are you looking forward to it?"

"Of course I am. It can't be soon enough for me."

She came to him then and ran her fingers through his hair. "I'm looking forward to it, too, believe me, honey." She bent and kissed him and his arms went around her, holding her as in a vise, his hands exploring the softness of her back. She stayed like that for a little while, then gently she released herself. "Johnny. There's something I want you to do for me."

"Anything, honey. Anything at all. Just name it."

"It's about those documents."

Instantly he was on the alert. "Yes?"

"I want you, as the logical person, to 'discover' the fact that I own the land on which they expect to lay their boulevard and water mains and sewer. Sort of casually call their attention to it. Will you do that?"

He was silent for a long time, his heart hammering in his chest. "I—I don't know, Nym."

"You don't know?"

"I should never have done what you asked. I never should have put them back."

Nym tried to hide her exasperation. She forced her voice to be calm. "Johnny, I took you into my confidence. I could simply have given you the deeds and asked you to return them for me. You could have done so and never been the wiser. But I told you why I needed your help. I trusted you. You are part of this deal. Part and parcel. You can't back out now."

"I want to, though, Nym." Johnny rose and came to her. He put his arms about her and held her close. "Look, Nym. You don't need the money you will be able to extort from them for that land. You've got plenty. Let's get those deeds and change them back again. Let's try to forget that we ever got involved in anything crooked. We can have a wonderful partnership without anything like that."

Nym almost gave herself away as a foul curse rose to her lips. But she did not utter it. She twisted out of his arms, knowing that such a response would disturb him greatly. She forced tears to her eyes. When she spoke, her voice was an intense whisper. "I've got to do it, Johnny. You must understand that. I'll never have peace until I have proved my superiority over men in this business. Until I have played at their own dirty game and won."

"You have the wrong idea about businessmen, Nym."

She laughed an ugly laugh. "Do I really? Oh, Johnny, you have lived in a cocoon all your life. You have no idea what they are like. Believe me, I know."

He walked away from her and sat on the edge of the large desk. "I can't do it, Nym. I just can't. Ever since I did the other thing for you it has tormented me, almost driven me crazy. I never did anything like that before. It is fraud and it is flagrantly dishonest. It makes me sick with guilt."

Nym followed him and stood very close to him, her hands resting on his shoulders. She forced him to look her in the eyes. "Do just this one more thing. For me, Johnny? Because it is so important to me? It isn't the money. It's the triumph that I want. Please help me. You have already helped me so much. Just do that one little thing more for me." She moved closer and brushed the sweeping curve of her thighs against him. "You won't ever be sorry, I promise you that," she whispered. "It's such a little thing. All you have to do is call their attention to my deed and to their own. That's all. They will take care of the rest." She moved her body slightly against his. "Please?"

Finally his face softened. "Let me think about it, Nym. Give me a little time, please."

"Then you will do it?"

"Maybe. But I must think about it first."

"Just don't think about it too long, will you, darling? You will be leaving the Register's office in two short weeks." It was a tremendous effort for Nym to control her impatience.

"I know. Just give me a coupe of days."

"All right, honey. A couple of days." She bent her head to his and pressed her mouth avidly against his lips. His hands slid almost mechanically down her back until the fingers were digging into the soft flesh of her hips. His eyes seemed to glaze over and she was satisfied that she still had control over the situation.

Neither of them noticed when the door behind them opened and Lynn, for a long moment, stood framed in the opening, her face frozen in a mask of horror and revulsion.

After Johnny had left, Nym returned to her desk in the outer office. She paid no attention to the other girl, but picked up some papers pertaining to a pending sale of some property. She sat staring at these. She did not read them, for her mind was on other things. She couldn't, she just couldn't start having trouble with Johnny now. He had to come through. She wracked her brain for ways of keeping him in line, but all she could think of was the same old way and for a brief instant she thought with pleasure, even with admiration, of her own body and her skill with it. She wondered vaguely how many other women were making their way in the world by using their bodies as instruments of progress. She figured there must be a lot of them.

She did not notice when Lynn first spoke. So the blonde girl repeated what she had said in a louder tone of voice.

"How could you, Nym!"

Nym looked up from the papers. "What?"

"How could you?"

"How could I what?"

"I saw you."

"You saw what, for heaven's sake?"

"I saw you and Johnny Martel in there."

"So?"

"What kind of a question is that? So? So I saw you, that's all. I saw just how much I mean to you!"

Nym sighed and rose from her desk. "You're a fool—a little damned fool!" she said and walked out of the office into the street.

At the Bijou Bar she sat down in a dark corner and ordered a highball. When it was brought to her, she held the frosty glass between her palms and sank into a deep reverie.

Things were not going right. They were not going right at all. She had thought her relationship with Lynn would be just a fleeting thing of pleasure, enjoyed by both without being taken seriously. The affair was actually of no importance at all to her. But now it loomed over her and kept interfering at the most unexpected moments, when her mind was on other things. It occurred to her that she had better get rid of Lynn. But she feared stepping on the girl's toes. The way Lynn appeared to feel, there was no telling what she might do if she were just simply dismissed. On the other hand, Nym could not allow her to keep nagging and disturbing the equilibrium of things. Nym tried to shrug the problem off, but it stuck in her consciousness, gnawing at her.

Then there was Johnny. He had been docile enough when she had told him about the documents and asked him to return them to the files. She had had no idea that what she considered such a simple action would assume such proportions in his conscience. It seemed that she had reckoned without Johnny's great and inherent honesty. He had seemed so easy to her the day he had come walking into the Bijou Bar and thus offered himself as the solution of an apparently insoluble problem. But now he was no longer easy. His was a clean and forthright mind. She had launched him on a road of misery which she now realized was extremely dangerous for her, because she could not foretell where it might lead. She had to maintain control by means of his love for her, to such an extent that he would walk that road blindly, allowing himself to be guided by her.

And Nym, her mind ever set on achieving her final triumph over the world of men—set on beating them at what she, in her blind distrust, considered "their own game"—found herself frustrated and hemmed in by the people who now constituted her life instead of Sean. She had expected such wonderful release in her hard-earned freedom, such great opportunities for carrying out her vindictive schemes, and instead she found herself chained and surrounded on every side.

I can't do it, he thought desperately. I simply can't.

Johnny buried his face in his hands, oblivious to the presence of the red-haired girl who stood by the window across his living room looking at him with worried eyes. I won't be able to live with myself for the rest of my life, he thought.

He lowered his hands and stared at the rush carpeting under his feet. What am I going to do? What am I going to do?

Just under his heart, in the inverted V of his solar plexus, there was a great, solid lump of fear and tension. He felt vaguely nauseated. I'll lose her. I'll lose Nym if I don't do it. I don't know what will happen to me if I lose her. I've waited all my life for her.

And Mickey, what about Mickey? Why don't I have the guts to tell her? What am I doing to her? Damn it, what is this thing that Nym has turned me into? A thing of mixed-up love and hate and fear and guilt! How long can I live like this?

He did not hear Mickey when she crossed the floor toward him. He did not look up and see how her eyes were filled with pity. He only noticed her presence when she took him gently by the hand and brought him to his feet.

"Come with Mickey," she said softly. "Come with Mickey. She'll make you feel better."

He was astonished at the compassion in her voice. How much did she suspect? How much did she know?

Regardless of what Mickey suspected or knew or felt, her love for Johnny was not dead entirely, and in the manner of women, she knew a way to give him at least momentary peace. She led him into his own bedroom, where the late afternoon sun was slanting its rays through the Venetian blinds. She brought him to the bed and undressed him as if he were a child and looked down at his still, unhappy face.

Then slowly she began to undress. She unzipped the side of her cotton dress and pulled it over her head. It was followed by the slip and she stood revealed in pale green bra and panties.

She unsnapped the strap of the brassiere and shrugged it from her shoulders and her full breasts swung free, their pink eyes crinkled and dormant against the white, white skin. She leaned over Johnny.

Johnny's face was smothered in her quivering flesh as he sucked the scent of her into his lungs. Little by little the painful imagery of evil was blotted from his mind.

Then Johnny soared off into that ecstasy which alone can cure all pain.

When it came to love, Mickey Stanton was a shameless woman.

CHAPTER SIX

The following morning two widely separate events, both of them of enormous importance to Nym Bardolph, took place.

Jock went back to the office of the Register of Deeds.

Sean O'Sullivan returned to Okeechee.

Tiny Gordon did not say anything for a long time after Jock brought him the unpleasant news. He simply stared out into the courtyard which seemed to be the source of all his inspirations. Finally he asked quietly, "Are they phony?"

Jock shrugged. "I don't know, Tiny. I got a brief glance at them, that's all. They looked all right to me, but only an expert could guarantee that."

"No wonder she was so anxious to sit on 'em for a little while. Them deeds are dynamite."

Then Mr. Gordon, his huge hulk sinking into itself until it looked like a monster octopus with its tentacles curled under it, retreated once more into silence. It was an uncomfortable silence, for it was not a peaceful one. Scheming was inherent in it, and ruthlessness and complete determination.

When Tiny finally spoke again, his mind was still on his first suspicion. "You wanna lay me odds they're phony?"

Jock laughed shortly. "Not me. Although I'll tell you something—that dame is not on the level a large percentage of the time, but I doubt whether she'd attempt forgery."

Gordon snorted contemptuously. "An' you claim you know something about people! That dame will stoop to anything if it'll get her what she wants. She prowls the business jungle like a damned tiger. Okay then, we'll treat her like a tiger. If she's hanging on to that land it's because she wants something out of it. An' I imagine it's dough she wants—what the hell else could it be? Well, we'll go offer her some dough. Tomorrow morning first thing."

And that just showed how wrong Mr. Tiny Gordon could be. For money had nothing to do with what Nym Bardolph wanted...

Sean O'Sullivan swung the station wagon out into the highway from the motel where he had spent the night. The tourist court was ten miles north of Okeechee and he had plenty of time to think as he wheeled along the road.

He cursed himself for a fool. Why had he come back? When he had left Nym and the town behind him, he had realized that it had been a long time since he had loved the ferocious woman whom he had tricked into marrying him. He had reconciled himself to the fact that the trick had not worked—that instead of learning to love him, as he had hoped she would, she had learned to hate him, and not only him but all men, because of what had been done to her mother and her, the crowning blow of which had been his own desperate act of coercion.

As he had driven north that morning nearly a month ago, how he had cursed himself! Let that be a lesson to you, you fool. You cannot teach love or buy love or trick love. You earn it. You cannot start earning love through blackmail.

At the same time, in partial vindication of himself, he had thought with bitterness of the fact that she was not a natural woman. What she had done to him during the last eight years far exceeded anything he had done to her. She seemed bent not only on destroying him, which she had already done, but on destroying herself.

He had driven to Jacksonville and gotten drunk that night. From Jacksonville he had gone to New Orleans, from New Orleans to St. Louis.

But nowhere did he find peace. Everywhere he went he looked at the little towns and the big cities and asked himself, do I want to start over again here and live here the rest of my life?

And always the answer was no.

Finally he turned the car around and headed south again. He drove night and day until he was almost back in Okeechee. Then he stopped and slept.

And now as he drove the final ten miles he asked himself, why have I come back?

The answer was very simple. He could not let Nym make the final ruination of herself and the name she bore through marriage to him by this filthy little fraud which she had perpetrated. Even if she got away with it, which seemed possible, he would know what she had done, would know that she had ruined herself as a woman, a person.

Nym was in the office when he arrived. She did not move from the desk, but sat quietly, staring at him as though he were a ghost.

He turned to the blonde secretary. "Do me a favor, will you, Lynn? Take a little walk."

The girl got up. "Oh sure," she said bitterly. "Sure, why not? Who am I?" She hurried out of the office into the street, and Sean realized with astonishment that she was crying as she went.

He turned to Nym. "What's the matter with her?"

"Nothing."

"She never acted like that before."

"Well, she acts that way now." Nym's voice was belligerent.

He sat on the corner of her desk. "Hello, Nym."

"Hello."

"How're things?"

"What do you want?"

"I'd like to talk to you, if I may. May we go into the inner office?"

"What's wrong with here?"

"What I've got to say is kind of private."

"Nobody is looking over your shoulder."

"Okay, then." He rose and walked a little away from her. "Where are those two deeds, Nym?"

"They're back where they belong."

"In the files in the courthouse?"

"That's right."

"But ... but how did you get them back there?"

"Oh, you're not as indispensable as you might think."

"I said, how did you get them there?"

"I've got friends."

"Friends? Who?"

"What's the matter with you? Don't you believe I have any friends?"

"Come off it, Nym. That's not what I'm asking. I want to know who returned those deeds."

"Suppose I don't tell you?"

"I'll find out."

"Why should you?"

"All right then, tell me something else. Did you alter them?"

"I did."

Sean took a deep breath and turned away from her. He stared out into the street, but saw nothing. Finally he spoke. "So you've sucked somebody else in on this deal."

"I didn't say that."

"You couldn't have gotten those papers back without arousing all sorts of suspicion. You're a real estate dealer and the wife of a councilman. You wouldn't have dared take them up there. So who did?"

"My new partner."

He whirled on her then. "Your—your what?"

"You heard me."

"Partner?" He looked about the office. "In this business?"

"Why not? It's not your business."

He moved closer to her, his eyes on her face, and he suddenly realized that he feared her. He feared her ruthlessness, her irresponsibility. He feared the evil which had grown like a cancer in her. He feared her and he hated her.

"Who is it?" he hissed.

She smiled. "Johnny Martel."

Sean's face blanched and he sank into the nearest chair. "He's one of the nicest boys in town," he breathed.

She rose to her feet. "You're insulting me," she snarled.

Sean looked at her wearily. How low could a woman stoop? "Am I?" he asked. "Is that really possible?"

"Johnny was anxious to go in with me. He has loved me ever since we were children."

"What has that got to do with it? What do you want to ruin him for?"

"Ruin him? This is the biggest chance of his life."

Sean spoke very slowly. "You're sick, Nym. Really sick. Please, for your own sake, don't do this crazy thing! Get hold of those documents. I'll go and get them for you. Change them back again and forget the whole thing. Please, let's start over again, Nym. And let's try to make everything right this time."

Nym Bardolph laughed.

Sean rose slowly to his feet and went out into the blinding glare of the street. He was hardly aware of where he was walking, nor was he conscious of the stares of passersby who were surprised at seeing him back in town.

Without any knowing effort on his part, his feet carried him to the courthouse and up the steps and down the hall. He did not actually recognize where he was until he stood in front of Johnny Martel's desk and saw the young man's startled eyes.

"Johnny," he said softly and humbly, "I'd like to talk to you for a minute, if I may."

Every look in the office was turned on him and he grew suddenly aware of this and began sweating uncomfortably. "Could we go somewhere?" he asked.

Johnny rose silently, his face expressionless, and followed Sean from the room. They went down the hall and into the street. Without saying a word they entered Johnny's car and drove to his apartment. Mutely they climbed the stairs and Johnny opened the door with his key and they went inside.

"Drink?" Johnny asked mechanically.

"That might not be a bad idea."

The young man went out to the kitchen while Sean looked around in a disinterested way. The boy had good taste. The small apartment was bright and modern and excellently decorated. Here and there Sean thought he detected the hand of a woman, though it was obvious that it was not Nym's hand. Then he remembered the handsome redhead he had seen Johnny with on a number of occasions.

Finally Martel returned with a highball in each hand. He gave one to Sean and sat down opposite him and lowered his eyes to the floor.

He's like a boy in the principal's office, Sean thought.

For a long time neither of them spoke. Then Johnny drew a deep, shuddering breath. "I expect I know why you're here," he muttered.

"I doubt it."

The boy looked up, startled.

"I mean if you think I am here to berate you or challenge you or name you as correspondent or something equally melodramatic, you're wrong. I'm here for an entirely different reason."

Sean almost smiled when he saw the stupefied look on the boy's face. "I don't want Nym—ever again—if that's what you're wondering. No, there's something entirely different that I want."

The boy, still completely bewildered, said, "What is that?"

"I want you to get those documents out of that file, fix them up right, and stop helping Nym commit forgery."

Johnny rose to his feet uncertainly. He went to the window and stared down into the sunny Florida street. "And if I refuse?"

"I'll expose you."

"You'd do that to your own wife?"

"She's not much of a wife to me at the moment."

Johnny lowered his eyes.

Sean interjected quickly, "Oh, don't think that I blame you. Don't ever think that. I spent a number of years as the victim of her wiles myself. I'm not apt to forget that. You're being played for a sucker, Johnny. For a real old-fashioned-a-number-one-sucker. She's very good at that."

"I love her." The statement was very simple, very straightforward.

"I know that. I loved her myself."

"This is different. I've loved her since we were children together."

"But does she love you?"

"Yes, she does."

"What makes you so sure of that?"

"She's told me."

"Oh?" Suddenly Sean was laughing.

Fury flared up in Johnny's face. "There's nothing funny about it. I believe her."

"So did I, on occasion."

"What does that mean?"

"She used to tell me she loved me when she wanted something out of me."

The boy's face turned sullen. "This is different," he repeated.

"Is it different enough to commit fraud for?"

The question struck home and Johnny's face was crossed with suffering. "I don't know," he muttered. "I don't know."

"Listen to me, Johnny. Nothing—not a single thing in the world—is worth an evil, cancerous conscience for the rest of your life."

"I can't help myself."

Sean rose and moved to stand next to the boy. He put a hand on his shoulder, but Johnny pulled away as though the touch were leprous. "Fight it, Johnny," Sean muttered. "Fight it with everything in you. She's no good, believe me."

The young man whirled away. "How can you say that? How dare you say that? She's the most beautiful, the tenderest..." He began to cry and Sean was bitterly disgusted with himself for having left town and exposed this youngster to the wiles of Nym. Had he not left, Nym would never have dared sink her claws into Johnny Martel.

"But she's a forger, Johnny. She's a criminal. Do you want to live with that?"

"Leave me alone. If I have to get my hands a little dirty to win her, I'm willing. She'll wash them clean."

"Do you really believe that?"

Now Johnny faced him squarely. "Yes, I believe it. Nym is not evil. This is the only wrong thing she will ever do. But this one thing she must do, or she will never be able to live with herself. She has some kind of idea of the wickedness of the world and she wants to beat wickedness with wickedness. When she has done that in this dirty deal she'll come to me and I will teach her what you never could, namely that she is wrong. And I will give her happiness which you never could. It's a happiness she deserves. And if it takes this to win it for her I will help her and I will be glad I did. Is that clear?"

Sean turned away from the ferociousness of the onslaught. Behind his back he heard the quick steps of the young man and he braced himself for the attack he fully expected. But Johnny ran to the door and tore it open and his footsteps echoed down the stairs. Sean was alone.

He had no idea, later on, how long he sat in that bright, cheery apartment, staring at the wall, his drink forgotten, everything forgotten except the searing terror in him.

During that hour, or those two hours or three or four, he fought a stout battle with himself. He knew as well as Nym the ugly circumstances of their marriage. He blamed himself now as much as she blamed him. But now it seemed too late to correct matters.

Perhaps Johnny was right Perhaps, now that he, Sean, was out of her life, she would do this one thing more and then find happiness with a boy her own age, a young man who had never hurt her. Perhaps through Johnny she could find peace. And Sean found himself wishing that she would find peace, for he had loved her once to the point of mania, and such love—though it may go dormant—lives on forever.

He wanted to believe this. At the same time he knew that he could not. And there were other responsibilities. He was a member of the City Council, even as young Johnny Martel was. They both had a duty to the town. But both were deeply involved in a crime against the very town for which they worked.

Sean knew what he ought to do. He ought to get up, go downstairs, walk to the mayor's office and tell him what he knew.

But Nym was still his wife. And perhaps…perhaps this would indeed be the last time, and then Nym would find peace.

Still, it would cost the city thousands of dollars…

Sean did not hear the door open, nor did he hear the gasp of startled fright that burst from Mickey Stanton as she entered the room. But when her suddenly trembling fingers slammed the door behind her, he looked up as if suddenly awakened from a dream.

Mickey stood just inside the living room, her eyes wide and frightened, and Sean thought abstractedly how lovely she looked, how fresh and clean and somehow innocent.

He jumped to his feet and the swift movement frightened her even more than his quietness of a moment before. She gave a little cry and pulled back against the door.

In his confusion he did not quite know what to say. "I—I beg your pardon," he stammered. "I … didn't mean to startle you. I am—"

"I know who you are," she said.

"I mean … I was talking to Johnny and he left and I just sort of got to thinking …" He realized abruptly that this lovely girl was involved in the matter, too. She was Johnny's fiancée, and whatever happened to Johnny and to Nym happened to her. It complicated the matter further.

"You were talking to Johnny?" she asked, coming into the room now, her obvious fear wearing off a little, but a new apprehension finding its way into her eyes. "What about?"

He did not know what to tell her. How much did she know? "Oh … about … about …"

"Johnny and your wife?"

"You know?"

"I know."

He said, "Won't you sit down?" Then he realized that this was not his apartment. He smiled apologetically. "I mean—I guess you have a good deal more right here than I have."

"Let me get a drink," she said and went out into the kitchen.

Sean looked at the door as it closed behind her and realized that this girl, whose name he did not even know, was very much a part of the horrible design of evil and misfortune that was shaping up. He found himself wondering what she was like and how she felt about this dreadful mess.

When she returned she was quite composed. She sat down on the couch, holding her drink carefully so that the condensation on the glass would not drop on her clean, starched summer dress. Sean noticed how well its aqua hue went with the flaming color of her hair.

He went back to his chair, but before he sat down he said hesitantly, "I'm sorry, miss … I don't even know your name … and I guess I really ought to, since we seem to be in this together."

"My name is Michelle Stanton," she said softly, "but everybody calls me Mickey. You can call me that, if you want to."

Sean felt very old. Very old indeed. Both Mickey and Johnny had about them a quality of youth that their contemporary, his wife Nym, had never had. They could both grin like youngsters, he was sure, although he had never seen it. He did know that they could sulk like youngsters and be bewildered and unsure of themselves and desperately lost and unhappy like youngsters. There was something reassuring in it, for it showed that they were not yet callous or ruthless or hardened in evil.

She looked at him and Sean saw that she was close to tears. "What were you talking to Johnny about, Mr. O'Sullivan?" she insisted.

"Please call me Sean. Well, I'm not sure myself right now just what I was talking to him about. When I started the conversation I felt very noble and very righteous, and also very right. When the talk was finished I was no longer so sure. Johnny told me some things about my wife that I had never considered. Perhaps I should ask what you think."

"I don't know what to think. I only know I have lost Johnny."

"Do you blame Nym?"

"Oh, I don't know. Should I? Johnny is a grown man. He must make his own decisions, his own choices."

"He has loved my wife since they were children."

"Yes, I know that now, although I did not know it a few days ago. If that is true, I can't hope to compete with her. In fact, I'm not even sure that I want to. Johnny is not like he used to be, any more."

"I can imagine that's true."

"Yes, I expect you know what I mean—better than I do myself."

Sean rose from his chair. "I'm sorry, Mickey, sorrier than I can tell you."

"Thank you, Sean. It doesn't help much."

"It might, one of these days," he said. "I hope to see you again."

And as he left the apartment, he bent over her where she sat on the couch and kissed her forehead.

Mickey did not move at all.

CHAPTER SEVEN

Nym had been badly shaken by Sean's brief visit. She did not know where he was staying and she did not know when she might see him again. She spent a restless night, tossing and turning in her bed.

Finally she got up, completely alone in the big house. She wandered down to the living room and fixed herself a drink. It occurred to her that she was beginning to lean on liquor, something she had never done before. But she shrugged it off and spent the early gray hours reading a magazine and sipping a highball.

When it came time for her to go to the office she hesitated a long while before dressing and going out. She did not think she could stand seeing Sean again. She knew that if she did she might break down, and all of her plans would be ruined. She was sick for Sean and sick over what she had done to him. She knew it now for sure.

But she stiffened her backbone and forced herself to consider the situation in the light in which she had grown used to considering it. She thought of her mother and she thought of what had happened to her mother—at the hands of her husband and at the hands of other men after Nym's father had died. She thought of what had happened to herself, of how Sean had forced her to marry him. She thought of the smug gentlemen on the City Council and how she was going to cook their collective goose.

But none of it gave her any satisfaction.

If I see Sean again today, I'll break, she thought, and she hated herself for her weakness. But her thoughts went on. Perhaps I want to see Sean. Perhaps I want to break. And she realized that this was true.

She dressed carefully, putting on the pale yellow underwear that she knew Sean loved, after bathing and powdering herself until she smelled like a fragrant flower garden. If I see him, she thought, I'll ask him to come home and I will make it all up to him. All of it!

But on the way to the office, driving recklessly as though she did not care what might happen to her, she saw no one but Johnny. She drew up to the curb—and admitted to herself that she wished she had never gotten involved with him. It also entered her mind that now, perhaps, it was too late for her to have such qualms.

Johnny got into the car and she gave him a ride down to the courthouse. He said very little, but after a while she asked, "Did Sean seek you out yesterday?"

He gave her a curt nod.

"What did he say?"

"If you had answered your phone last night, I could have told you then."

"I didn't feel well."

"Really?"

"Don't be nasty, Johnny. I felt ill. No matter what you think."

"Because your husband came home?"

"He was not with me."

"Then where is he staying?"

"I haven't any idea."

"You mean he really was not with you?"

"That's exactly what I mean, Johnny."

Then he was like a little boy—all contrition. "I ... I thought he was. I'm sorry."

"He and I are through, Johnny." Even as she said it she knew that she hoped it was not so.

"He knows all about us, Nym."

"Of course he does."

"What do you suppose he's going to do?"

"What did he say to you?"

"Nothing. Nothing of any importance."

"Is that the truth?"

"We don't trust each other very much, do we?"

"No ... perhaps we don't, Johnny."

"He—he warned me against you."

That hurt. That hurt Nym way down deep, although she knew that she had earned it. "I see."

"What are we going to do?"

"What about you, Johnny? What are *you* going to do? Are you going to do what I asked you? Once that is done, there won't be a problem any more."

"I don't know. I don't know, Nym. I've got to think."

"You don't really love me, do you, Johnny?"

"Oh, that's not so. You know that is not so, darling. I'll do anything for you. Anything!"

"Well?"

"Give me time, Nym."

"Time is running out."

She pulled up the car in front of the courthouse and Johnny got out. She watched him as he went up the steps. Then she called him back. "Don't call me today, Johnny, or come by the office. I'd like to have a little time to myself."

His resentment was quick and hot. "You meeting Sean?"

"No, Johnny."

"Then why?"

"I just want a little time to myself."

"Are you by any chance cutting me off because I won't do what you ask of me?"

"No, honey, that's not it. Oh, I don't know what it is. Just don't call me or come by, that's all. I'll call you tomorrow."

"Promise?"

"I promise."

He went off again, looking more like a petulant little boy than ever, and Nym turned her car down the street toward her office.

She did not know why she had sent Johnny packing today. Perhaps she was hoping that Sean would turn up. Perhaps she *was* putting a little pressure on Johnny in order to get him going with those documents.

No, she was sure that was not it. Had she not promised herself that if Sean turned up she would call off the whole deal? Then how could she, at the same time, be pressing it toward a climax?

A shock was in store for her at the office.

Tiny Gordon was waiting for her there. Enthroned in the same spindly chair in which he had sat once before, he looked monstrous and gelatinously protoplasmic. Standing beside him and almost dwarfed by his ghastly bulk was a small, wizened man of indeterminate age.

Lynn was nowhere in evidence.

Tiny grinned engagingly. "The janitor let us come in and set, ma'am," he said and struggled to his feet, wheezing and puffing.

Nym went into the room. She removed her trim jacket while she murmured a good-morning and went to the chair behind her desk.

But before she could sit down the enormous man said softly, in a tone of deep conspiracy, "Perhaps we could talk in private, Mrs. O'Sullivan? Could we go into the other office?" He nodded his head toward the door in the back wall. "Oh," he continued contritely, as if he had forgotten his manners, "this here's my lawyer, mmmmmmm..." and he muttered an unintelligible name.

Nym nodded pleasantly and said, "Certainly." She led the way into the inner room, the two men following her closely.

"Now," she asked after they had found chairs, "what can I do for you this time, Mr. Gordon?"

"Well, Mrs. O'Sullivan, it's hard to say. You know how it is; some of us fellers don't give up so easy. As a matter of fact, it's still a matter of that same land up north of town."

"You remember what I told you, sir. The land is not for sale."

"Now, Mrs. O'Sullivan, you cain't really be meaning that. You didn't have them deeds out of the Register's office for more than ten days just to be takin' inventory—did you?"

"Yes, I did, Mr. Gordon." She became aware quite suddenly that the fat man's eyes seemed to be cutting right into her, and a crazy impulse to cover her breasts with her hands filled her for an instant. It was as if he were penetrating to her nakedness and leering at it. But it was not really the nakedness of her body he was leering at, it was the nakedness of her mind.

A little smile was on his rosebud mouth, a guileless smile, a smile of boyish innocence. "I take it from that answer, Mrs. O'Sullivan, that it was not just your own deed which you had out, but also the other one to which I referred the other day."

Nym realized with a sickening feeling of horror that by her thoughtless answer she had given herself away. "I … I don't know what … you m-mean," she stammered.

The smile was still on Gordon's swollen face. "I mean the city's deed, of course, ma'am. You know, the one you had out together with your own."

Nym knew he was watching her like a hawk, searching for the slightest tremor. How much does he know, she thought frantically. What is he looking for? Has he just guessed, or has he had the papers checked by an expert?

Again, and this time like a little girl longing for her father's helping hand, she thought of Sean. Oh, why did she ever get into this? She was frightened beyond any fright she had ever experienced before.

Why, you're a coward, she contemptuously accused herself. When the chips are down, you're a coward. She fought desperately to keep from showing her fear. Holding her voice in meticulous control, she said, "To tell you the truth, I was simply checking one against the other, Mr. Gordon. There is nothing sinister at all about my having had both deeds out."

"My gracious me, ma'am, whoever said anything about it being sinister? I am merely interested in a possible purchase of your land. What might be your price on it now?"

"There isn't any price, Mr. Gordon."

The huge man laughed, and once again, even in her fear, Nym was amazed to see the ocean waves of laughter rolling across his flesh, as though he were not of solid bulk but rather a mass of liquid. "You're a mighty hard woman to deal with, Mrs. O'Sullivan," he finally gasped. "Could you be having a reason for holding out on them eighteen acres? Could you be knowing something about them that I don't? Could you, now?"

The innocence in the man's voice, coupled with the insinuation of hidden knowledge, confused Nym. She tortured her mind to try to figure out whether he knew nothing at all, or whether he knew a little and was trying to bait her out into the open, or whether he knew everything and was openly threatening her.

"I don't know what you are hinting at, sir," she said rather curtly. "There's nothing unusual in a realtor's checking his or her assets. And the land up there is not for sale."

The smile disappeared from Tiny Gordon's face. "That is your final word?"

"It is."

He heaved his bulk from the chair he had been filling to overflowing. "Mrs. O'Sullivan, I'm going to be frank with you. I always find it pays to be frank and above board, don't you? I want that land. I am willing to pay any price you care to set on it. Any price at all."

"I'm not going to set a price on it, Mr. Gordon."

"But why not, woman, for heaven's sake?" Mr. Gordon's exasperation was quite evident.

"I don't care to sell it. That's final, sir." Nym rose. "And now if you'll forgive me, I have a lot to do ..."

Tiny wheezed hastily, "Just a minute please, ma'am, I'm not quite finished. I had sort of hoped to avoid certain methods of trading, but you're forcing my hand. Ma'am, on the surface things don't look so good for you. Now please understand me—it would never occur to me that a lady like you could be guilty of a little skullduggery, but there might be others more gullible than I who'd get kinda startled if they knew what has been happening with them deeds."

Nym sat back down heavily. Her face turned white as chalk and unconsciously she folded her hands to keep them from trembling. Well, here it comes, she told herself, and the thought numbed her senses as if she had been injected with novocaine. She heard the voice of Tiny Gordon droning on.

"First of all, you're in the real estate business. Secondly, your husband is on the City Council. Does that connection ring a bell in your mind? Now, the City Council has just made a certain important decision pertaining to the territory north of the city. You're the only real estate dealer who could possibly know about that decision. Two deeds disappear from the files in the Register's office. Two very important deeds in this connection. Now ain't that a little peculiar? Deeds don't usually disappear from the files in that office. Particularly in such an interesting connection. Suddenly the deeds appear again and who knows but what a little something ain't been happening to them during their absence? Now, mind you, I ain't claiming that anything has. But the idea has got possibilities—now, ain't it? A story like that would look kinda bad, wouldn't it?"

"Go on, Mr. Gordon. It's your story, not mine." Nym wondered how much longer she could stand the tension of her terror without breaking. She sat very still and she was deeply aware of a strong trembling somewhere below her heart. It felt as though some living, organic manifestation of fear was lodged there.

"Well now, like I said, I'm going to be frank with you. Spreading that story around wouldn't do me good, because the city would never allow me to get my fingers on your land under such circumstances. Once your deed is made they're going to have to buy that land from you or prove that there has been skullduggery and just take it from you. But that wouldn't do me a bit of good, would it? So like I said, I'll be honest with you. I want that land mighty bad. I ain't no piker. Naturally, you're holding out to force the city to pay you whatever you demand when you've got 'em in such a public position that they can't back out on their plans. Tell me what you're expectin' them to shell out with, Mrs. O'Sullivan, and I'll jump the price five thousand dollars and no questions asked. Now ain't that a fair offer?"

Gradually Nym began to realize that her position in this, no matter what Tiny Gordon might know, or might think he knew, was not as untenable as it had looked for a little while. The realization brought her senses back under control again, and little by little the fear began to drain from her. She stirred a bit restlessly where before her body had been frozen as a statue. She even managed a little smile.

"Very well, Mr. Gordon, you've been frank with me. I'll be frank with you. It's not the money I'm after. Any price you might be willing to pay would mean absolutely nothing to me. No, Mr. Gordon, I have a score to settle with the fine gentlemen on the City Council. That is why I am holding out."

She saw the surprise and the dismay settle in the fatty folds of his enormous face. This was a man, and she had rocked him back on his heels. She waited for the pleasure which heretofore she had always experienced in such moments. But the pleasure was not forthcoming. She shook her head slightly, and sighed.

"What have you got against the City Council, ma'am?" he asked in utter astonishment.

"They're men," she answered quietly.

"Men?" He seemed a little awed, as if the problem were so far beyond his comprehension that it appeared to him to have certain metaphysical qualities about it.

"I wouldn't expect you to understand." Her voice was curt.

"No, ma'am. I'll be the first to admit that I don't."

"Anyway, that's my reason. It has nothing to do with money."

Gordon rose from his chair and towered over the still-seated Nym. He wrung his hands awkwardly and there was a pleading note to his tone. "Ma'am," he began uncomfortably, "you know very well that the days of land-grabbing are gone. I cain't just move in on your land and push you off it. I cain't sow no seeds of suspicion in the minds of people in the courthouse, 'cause that ain't gonna get me nowhere. I want that land. Okay, there's only one way for me to get it and that is through a fair and square and legitimate sale-and-purchase, with all the papers signed, sealed, and delivered. Now Tiny Gordon has got a name for getting what he wants. Is there anything at all that will make you interested in selling?"

Nym was smiling broadly at the man's obvious discomfort. "No, Mr. Gordon, there isn't. I'm almost beginning to feel sorry for you, you seem to want it so bad."

Tiny was almost weeping. "Ma'am, you're gonna feel sorrier, 'cause I just simply cain't give up this deal. Please, ma'am, don't force me to use persuasion. I hate it, Mrs. O'Sullivan. I hate it real bad. I have been known to use it on very extreme occasions, but I tell you, I can't hardly sleep or eat for days afterwards."

Now Nym rose too, her eyes flashing angrily. This sort of thing she expected from men. She had come to expect it through twenty-six years of life during which men, when they did not instantly get what they wanted, had resorted to threats. It almost pleased her that Gordon had proved true to his ilk. She had felt weak before. She had felt frightened, and when she had had her little moment of triumph, her reaction had not been true to form. Now she felt at home again, on sure ground. This was something she knew how to handle.

"Get out, Mr. Gordon," she said briefly. "I was wondering when you would get around to this."

Gordon turned to the little wizened man, who had as yet said nothing at all, but had watched the proceedings through his little weasel-eyes with great curiosity and interest. "Jock," he wheezed, tears in his eyes, "Jock, talk to her! Tell her she's bein' a fool."

"Talking to this one isn't going to do you a bit of good, Tiny."

"But she's gotta understand. She's gotta understand that I mean it. She's gotta understand that when Tiny Gordon makes up his mind to something it happens, no matter how much it hurts him to do it. Please talk to her, Jock."

Nym found the fat man utterly ludicrous as he blubbered his threats and sniffled and wiped the tears from his eyes. She walked to the door and opened it and beckoned the men to leave.

They both walked out, Gordon wiping his face and hiding his tears with a huge red handkerchief.

She watched them disappear down the street, the fat and blubbering clown so ridiculous that she completely discounted his threat…

As the day wore on and Lynn never turned up at the office, Nym finally called the girl's home. She was informed that Lynn had gone out that morning and was not expected back until night. She hung up, vaguely wondering what had happened to the little blonde secretary.

Her mind, however, did not stay on the problem long, for she had other matters that had to be attended to. She realized now that no matter what she had said to Tiny Gordon she had no intention of going through with the deal involving the forged deeds. As she sat staring at the empty walls of the office she knew exactly what she was going to do.

She was going to close up the office, go out and find Sean, tell him that she had been wrong, ask him to come home, and then—together—they would straighten this whole mess out and live happily ever after.

That was what Nym Bardolph thought.

She rose from her place behind the desk, closed the office and strode out into the sun, her heart light and happy for the first time since she could remember. It was as if a great weight had fallen from her shoulders, and she rejoiced that Sean had come back and that he had come to see her the day before. She was sure that once she found him she could gain his forgiveness.

She got into the big car and drove off on her hunt for her husband.

She spent the remainder of the day searching the city, but nowhere was the man to be found. She tried every hotel and every tourist court and the homes of all their friends, but it was as if Sean had been swallowed up by the sandy earth. It was as if he had risen from the soil for a brief moment the day before and then returned from whence he came, leaving no single trace of ever having been in Okeechee. There were moments when Nym found herself doubting that she had actually seen him.

But she did not give up. When night came she returned to her home, intent on starting her search again tomorrow. Somewhere Sean was to be found, she knew, and when she found him everything was going to be all right.

She ran the car into the garage and walked across the shadowy yard and let herself into the house.

As she entered the pitch-dark hall, her arms were pinioned from behind by great hands that felt as though they were made of steel. She cried out once, but instantly a broad piece of tape was slapped across her mouth and she felt her wrists tied behind her back. Then she was pushed and shoved and dragged into the living room.

A soft voice that seemed to come from the man with the steel hands spoke from behind her back. "Turn the light on in the kitchen and leave the door partly open so we can make out what we're doing."

The light went on in the other room and a sharp beam fell through the half-open door in such a manner that the room was barely lighted. She could now make out the shapes of her tormentors. Their faces were carefully covered by masks. Nym recognized the masks as the grotesque rubber kind which can be bought in any five-and-dime. There were two men and she did not recognize them.

She was so frightened that she was afraid she was going to be sick. She took a mighty hold on herself and tried to stand up straight without trembling. She tried to speak, but the tape prevented her.

"Now, Mrs. O'Sullivan," said the man who had spoken before, "not a thing in the world is going to happen to you, if you'll just go to the trouble of signing this little paper."

As he held the document toward her so she could read it in the dim light, Nym marveled at the cultured tones of his voice. What could have made a man who was obviously educated stoop to this?

She read the typed paper. It was a simple agreement whereby she promised to sell the eighteen acres specified in her own deed to Frederick Gordon. She shook her head vigorously.

The man who was obviously the spokesman shook his head regretfully. "Please, Mrs. O'Sullivan," he said politely. "Don't do this to yourself. You know how Tiny hates it, too. So it is something you won't want and it is something Tiny doesn't want. Obviously it would be much more agreeable all around if you just signed and we parted like friends."

The mask he was wearing was a devil's head, and ludicrous as it looked, it lent a certain Mephistophelian air to him which was supplemented by the soft and cultured voice.

Nym's eyes were flashing now and he read the challenge in them correctly. "Mrs. O'Sullivan," he said politely, "I would think a number of times, if I were you, before reporting this little séance. You have not had a single witness to any of your meetings with Mr. Gordon, nor could you prove that what is about to happen to you—if you do not sign—is Mr. Gordon's doing. Besides, complaints stir up inquiries, and inquiries lay open secrets. Don't you have any secrets up in the courthouse which you would not like to have laid open? Please, ma'am, why don't you just sign and let's forget the whole thing."

Nym, strengthened now by her loathing and her fury, shook her head violently.

The man shrugged. He beckoned to his companion, a slightly smaller man, whose pale eyes glowed through the eyes of the mask of a grotesque and somehow obscene-looking pink pig. "Hold her arms for just a minute."

Nym felt her arms pinioned and tried again to scream, but the tape held her mute.

With terrible deliberation the man in the devil's mask slapped her several times across the face, and Nym felt the tears starting from her eyes with the pain. Then the slapping stopped.

"Now, ma'am, won't you please believe that we mean business?"

She gritted her teeth and shook her head once more.

The devil reached out, and calmly taking his time, slipped the jacket off her shoulders. It slid backward along her arms and fell over her wrists, hanging down to the floor behind her. Then he proceeded methodically to unbutton her blouse. Eventually it followed the jacket, and suddenly she felt the two garments being released from her wrists with the aid of a slitting jacknife.

The pig spoke from behind her. He had a hoarse, strained voice, as though he could hardly control his excitement. "Let's do it slow. Take the skirt next."

The devil said, "Any time you change your mind, ma'am, just nod your head and we'll quit right then."

"I hope she doesn't," said the pig, and his voice seemed to be licking its lips.

The devil's hands went to the waistband of her skirt.

Nym tried to knee him in the groin, but he spun out of the way in time. His hand struck her a stinging blow across the cheek. "Please don't do that, Mrs. O'Sullivan," he said politely.

She felt a leg go around her own legs from behind, and figuring that the pig-mask was standing on one leg, she tried to throw her weight forward to fling him off balance. If she could get free for just a moment, she could run out the front door and try to throw herself on the mercy of some passing motorist. Then she remembered her bound wrists. How was she going to open a door?

She did not succeed in throwing the man behind her off balance and she heard him chuckle softly, breathlessly. Then her waistband was undone and the skirt dropped about her feet. Her half-slip followed.

She was standing before the two men in the pale yellow brassiere and panties which were Sean's favorites and which she had put on for his benefit.

"You're a very beautiful woman," said the devil softly. "I wonder what you will look like without this." And he reached out suddenly and literally tore the brassiere from her breasts. The full, quivering globes sprang into view and she heard the convulsive intake of breath as the men saw them.

"It's a sin, Mrs. O'Sullivan, to do this to such a beautiful woman. Please sign and don't force us any further."

The pig grunted, "Don't urge her, you. You wanna stop the fun?"

"Tiny won't think it is fun if we have to go back and tell him how far we had to go. He won't be able to sleep for nights and nights."

"Ah, the hell with that. Get on with the business at hand."

"Mrs. O'Sullivan?" It was a polite query.

Nym shook her head.

Then suddenly the panties were ripped from her body with one violent sweep and she stood completely revealed in the soft light.

And then the devil-mask was no longer polite. Nym, her whole being pulsing with horror, her knees giving way under her until she was held upright only by the strength of the man behind her, heard his harsh breath as it whined its labored way through a passion-constricted throat. She felt his hands obscenely caressing her helplessly exposed body and for once she cursed the effect her body had on men.

She felt her torso being arched inexorably backward until she formed a tense, taut bow, completely helpless.

And now the devil-mask no longer pleaded with her to sign. Without another word he struck her with horrible accuracy in the chest and a horrid shriek rose in Nym's throat only to be stopped by the tape that bound her lips. Again and again he struck, his blows raining all over her exposed body with methodical thoroughness.

She felt herself thrown on the couch and in a red haze of dreadful pain she bucked and leaped under the stinging lash of the beating, no sound coming from her throat though she was screaming inside.

Finally, mercifully, she began to black out. When the men became aware of her growing limpness, they ceased their merciless work. And suddenly she felt herself turned onto her back and a glass of ice-cold water was thrown in her face. The freezing liquid revived her and she became again aware of the horrible fire in her back. It felt as though it had been flayed of skin and she was lying on her own raw, red flesh.

"Now?" the pig-face asked eagerly, like a comedian in a vaudeville show.

"Now." The answer was laconic.

She felt herself lifted and carried into the bedroom. Whoever was carrying her flung her to the bed.

She rolled her body frantically and silently, to no avail…

Many hours later Nym came to. She thought she was swimming and gently moved her legs to keep from going under. But then she realized that she was not surrounded by water. The water was concentrated in a little patch that slid soothingly over her breasts. She breathed deeply with a sigh of satisfaction. Then suddenly she felt the horrible pain in her back.

Crying out, she opened her eyes.

Lynn was leaning over her, nude and gleaming in the light from the bedside lamp. She was gently rubbing Nym with a cold, wet washcloth. Nym's mouth was no longer gagged. She saw that Lynn's eyes had a strange, wild gleam in them and that the girl looked as if she had been through hell—and hell had taught her something she had never known before.

Weakly Nym's hand went out and touched her. "Where did you come from?" she asked, her voice hoarse with pain.

Lynn looked straight into the agonized eyes. "I came out here tonight because I wanted to see you."

"But where have you been?"

"Walking. Walking for a whole day. After your husband came home yesterday, I didn't know what to do. Finally I just had to see you. So I came out here."

"When?"

"At five this afternoon."

Nym tried to sit up, but the pain threw her back and she gave a little strangled cry.

Lynn, her eyes momentarily losing their odd glitter and filling with compassion, bent forward and kissed her gently on the lips. "You poor, poor thing."

Nym finally caught her breath again. "You mean you were here all the time?"

"Yes."

"But... but why didn't you run for help or scream or something?"

"Because I wanted to see you get your beating. It was a beating you deserved."

Nym stared wide-eyed at the blonde whom she had never known as anything but kind and docile and unimaginative.

Lynn bent over again and nuzzled her gently. "You poor, poor thing," she murmured again.

CHAPTER EIGHT

Nym lay in her bed, triumphant. A seething mass of awful pain, she felt triumphant nevertheless. She had taken all they had to give and had not been defeated. Tiny Gordon and his men might be back, but she would never sign. She knew that now.

Forgotten were all her misgivings, all her remorse of yesterday. Her hatred of the race of man had grown to new, magnificent measure.

This was man, then. A predatory beast that pounced upon you in the night and tried by force and tooth and claw to extract from you anything you had that he might want. Your house, your business, your body and your soul.

Well, she would show them! Never again would she be weak and ready to crawl to any man as she had been yesterday. Sean was again an eight-year symbol of the fact that man can be beaten at his own game. Just that and nothing more. Nothing more at all.

Nym lay staring at the ceiling, her eyes gleaming with hatred, her whole being infused with fierce vindictiveness. Now she would never swerve from her purpose. She cursed herself for being a weakling and a fool even to have considered running to Sean.

Lynn came and went regularly. She bathed Nym's bruises and cooked her food and ministered to her needs. A great change had taken place in the little blonde too. She moved with a sureness and authority which she had never displayed before. Her eyes looked straight at the world without flinching, and now and then she seemed more like a mother to Nym than anything else.

Deep fires burned within her which were never again to be extinguished. Lynn was a woman now and walked straight-backed and fearless along strange and devious paths.

She was sitting by the bed, the two of them holding hands, when the doorbell rang and Lynn went to answer it.

It was Johnny Martel. Lynn tried to turn him away, but he pushed his way past her into the living room. "Where is she? I've got to see her. I can't stand being held off any longer. Why the hell doesn't she answer her phone?"

"Go away, Johnny. Nym is sick in bed."

"Sick?"

"You heard me. Go away and leave her alone. She doesn't want to see you."

"Why not? What have I done to her? Why shouldn't she want to see me?"

"Take my advice, Johnny, go away and don't ever come back."

He turned from her abruptly, and striding across the large room, he burst into the bedroom where Nym lay. He was horrified at what he saw. He stopped dead in his tracks and stared at the pale, puffed, bruised face, the blackened eyes, the swollen lips.

Then he rushed to the bed and fell to his knees beside it. "Nym, Nym!" he cried. "What has happened to you?"

Nym stared at him coldly and did not answer.

"Nym, darling. Tell me."

Nym turned her head away from him. She could not make herself speak to any man at the moment.

Lynn's voice spoke drily from the doorway. "She got beat up."

Johnny whirled where he was kneeling. "Beat up?"

"It was a beating she deserved. It has taught her a lesson. It has made everything better."

"What do you mean, better? Are you crazy or something?" He turned back to Nym. "Who did this? Who did this, Nym? Tell me, and so help me I'll kill him."

Lynn's voice was still dry. "It wasn't a *him*. It was a *they*."

Johnny spun again in fury. "Shut up, you, and get out of here."

Lynn came into the room. "I'm not going anywhere." Her voice was cold and hard as steel.

Johnny turned to Nym again. "Tell me, Nym. Do you hear? Who were they?" Then great tears began to roll down his cheeks and he bent forward until his head was touching her breast, and he sobbed, "You poor, poor thing!"

Nym's and Lynn's eyes met over his bent head, faint amusement mirrored in both their faces.

"You get a lot of sympathy," said Lynn, her voice fairly crackling with sarcasm this time.

But then a thought struck Nym. Now—if ever—was the time to strike, and make use of Johnny. She slid a weak arm about his neck and cuddled his face close against her bruised breasts. Lynn, observing the motion, stiffened, her face turning into a mask of hardness.

"Johnny, Johnny," Nym whispered. "Oh, Johnny, I'm glad you're here."

He raised his tear-stained face. "Who did this to you, Nym?" he asked, his voice stiff with his effort to control it.

She pulled him closer to her. "I can't tell you that, Johnny. All I can tell you is that it's someone who is trying to prevent me from carrying out my plans with the City Council."

"And this is the way they try to stop you?"

"Yes, Johnny."

"Tell me. Tell me who it is."

"Later, Johnny. But first there's something you must do for me. Go at once and show my deed to the mayor. If you don't do it now, it may be too late."

She saw the cloud pass over his face and pushed him away a little bit so that she could look into his eyes. "Go now, Johnny, if you don't want this to happen again. Go, Johnny, if you love me."

"If I love you! Nym, can you doubt that? I've been going crazy since you told me yesterday not to call you until you called me. Oh, Nym, Nym, I can't live without you!"

She ran her fingers through his short-cropped hair. "If you do this for me you will never have to live without me. I promise you, Johnny."

"Do you love me, Nym?"

"I love you, darling. Now please go before it is too late."

Johnny got to his feet and looked down at her, lying bruised and pitiful in the large bed. "I'll do anything for you, Nym. Anything. I want you to know that always. When I come back I want you to tell me who did this, do you hear?"

"When you come back, Johnny, we'll never be separated again." She saw the tears rising into his eyes again. Then abruptly he turned on his heel and strode from the room.

Nym looked at the other girl, a great satisfied smile broadening her features. "That takes care of that," she said, and now there was no longer any hesitation, any softness, any remorse in her.

Lynn stared her straight in the eyes, her face a mask of hatred. "You can go straight to hell," she muttered coldly and started out of the room.

Nym called her back. "Lynn, what's the matter?"

"That was a great little performance."

"But that's all it was, dear."

"Yes? I've seen you and him together before." Suddenly she came back until she was standing right over Nym.

"I could kill you," she hissed between her teeth. Then she whirled and left the room.

Her exit made no great impression on Nym. She'll be back, Nym thought.

When Nym woke up alone in the big house, the morning sun was slanting through the draperies at the windows. She tried to stretch and found that the sharp, stabbing pain in her back had turned into a dull ache. She could move a little now.

She eased herself out of bed and walked gingerly into the kitchen. She fixed herself a cup of coffee and then took a long, warm bath and dressed herself in a red velvet housecoat.

She lay down on the couch in the living room and waited for Johnny's return. She was not in the least nervous. She felt strong, determined, unbeatable in her hunger for revenge. She waited patiently.

It was ten o'clock before he came.

He was triumphant. "It went off without a hitch, Nym. Gosh, you should have seen the mayor's face! He stared and stared at those two deeds, he shifted them from hand to hand, he shuffled them and smoothed them and curled them over his fingers. He was flabbergasted. He called a meeting of the council last night and it was decided that no matter what price you ask, they must buy your land because of all the publicity and the recent land-boom out that way. There was never a question of the validity of the documents. They were just caught flat-footed and they all had to admit that they had been very slovenly indeed in not checking what they were sure the city owned. So name your price, darling, and enjoy this victory that you have always wanted."

Nym, although it hurt her to do so, sat up on the couch. Her lips were set in a straight line and her face looked almost satanic in its wild and uncontrolled expression of evil satisfaction. Finally she rose and started to pace around the room. Faster and faster she went, until she was almost running. "Don't you worry," she muttered, "I'll enjoy it, all right. I'll enjoy it. And this is just the beginning. Only the very start. I'll destroy this whole town. I'll tear it brick from brick until they come crawling to me for solace. Until they come puling and slobbering and begging me to stop. Until every mother's son of them has whined that he is licked."

Johnny watched her in horror. "Nym!" he cried. "Nym, what are you saying?"

She stopped and stared at him and her eyes gleamed with hatred. "You heard me..."

"But your promises, Nym? This was the last time. Never again. We are going to be happy together now and nothing like this will ever happen again. Don't you remember?"

"You whining slob," she said in utter and complete contempt.

"Nym, for heaven's sake! Listen to me. What has come over you?"

"Nothing that hasn't been there all the time."

"You mean all this time you have just been using me? You have been play-acting? Leading me on?"

She could see the fury growing in him and she loved the sight of it. Seeing a man that upset was better than seeing love in his face. It was better than making love. She reveled in it "That's right. I needed you. I used you. Just as men used me and my mother until we discovered how to strike back. Now get out of here. I don't need you any longer."

The terrible anger boiled out of him like a sudden burst of molten lava. "Do you think I'm going to let you get away with this? I'll expose you to the whole city."

Her voice dripped contempt. "Go ahead. You're up to your neck in it yourself. You wouldn't have the guts."

He stared at her, his anger subsiding for a moment. "And my love means nothing to you?" He waited for an answer, but received none. "Or our plans? Or the fact that I gave up everything for you and now I will have to live with this for the rest of my life? All that means nothing to you?"

Nym started to laugh. Her laughter wracked her aching body so that the muscles, painfully uncontrolled, expelled the sound in crazy, convulsive heaves.

"You're mad," he whispered. "Either mad or the most evil thing that ever lived." Then suddenly the great bubble of hurt burst within him. "And to think I might have lived with you. Like Sean I might have become a victim of your rotten mind."

His voice rose into hysteria. "I'll kill you," he screamed. "I'll kill you!"

And he rushed insanely from the room and out of the house.

When Nym stopped laughing she went back to bed and slept soundly until evening...

When she awoke again, the big house was quiet. It was night and she was very hungry.

Very well, she thought, I'll indulge myself tonight and celebrate a little. I'll take my dinner at the country club.

She got out of bed and found that her bruises did not hurt as much as they had that morning and not nearly as much as they had last night. She bathed again and dressed carefully in a chic little suit she had bought on a trip to Miami a couple of months earlier. She deliberately put on her oldest, most unattractive underwear.

Never again do I need to entice anyone with my underclothes or with my body, she thought. And she rejoiced at the idea.

The house seemed empty, but that too was pleasing. That was the way she wanted it now. Her whole being was filled with only one thing. There was nothing else. Only the hunger to go on and on and on until this awful parched thirst was slaked and she could find peace in the utter satisfaction of complete destruction. That was what being alone meant. And it was a good, strong, self-reliant feeling.

She finally left the house and drove off in the big car.

CHAPTER NINE

Mickey Stanton, soft and beautifully rounded in her revealing negligee, peered down at Johnny. "I don't understand. I don't understand at all."

"There's nothing to understand."

Mickey shook her head, the lustrous red hair gleaming in the lamplight. "But won't you tell me what happened? Johnny, you can't do this to me. Won't you even talk?"

He remained silent. Mickey's concern touched him, and he wanted to put his arms around her, to console her, to alleviate the hurt he had caused her. But there was nothing he could do or say, nothing until the dragging agony deep inside him let go enough to ease his tormented mind. And the agony was there to stay.

Only one thing would remove it.

One thing, and it was not time yet.

"If you'd only sleep," Mickey said. "Can't you close your eyes and try? I'm frightened, Johnny. You've never been like this before." She came close and placed a solicitous hand on his forehead. "It feels hot. Are you sure you don't have a fever?"

"Fever?"

"Should I call a doctor?"

He smiled, and it was the first smile in a long time. "No, Mickey, don't call a doctor."

"But—"

"No." The cool fingers on his brow felt wonderful. He owed it to her, he owed this girl some kind of explanation.

Explanation?

No, he owed Mickey Stanton more than that. Mere words would never take the place of what she had lost. He had robbed this girl, robbed her as cruelly and brutally as if he had jammed a gun into her ribs and torn her heart from her bosom.

Just as Nym Bardolph had torn out his.

No. No, not torn. Sliced—neatly and efficiently sliced. Nym was too clever, too meticulous, too exact to tear or rip or get her hands messy. Every thought and movement was planned well in advance; only a poor blundering fool got blood on his hands. And Nym was neither poor nor blundering—and certainly not a fool. She had probed and cut and laid bare his vitals, and he felt as if every idea, every tiny quirk of her devious brain were a surgical scalpel. Each small slice had been only a little thing by itself, but now he could see all too clearly that it was all part of a pattern. Nym had reached inside him, inch by inch, just as deftly as a fine surgeon performing a major operation.

Great, he thought bitterly. The operation was a success but the patient died. Nym had used him and wrung him dry and now as far as she was concerned, he might just as well be a corpse ready to be planted in some nicely manicured graveyard. With a simple headstone, suitably engraved:

HERE LIES JOHNNY MARTEL.
STUPID JOHNNY MARTEL.
HE UNDERESTIMATED THE
POWER OF A WOMAN.

And perhaps a few flowers, brought and irrigated daily by the tears of the girl who really loved him. The girl whose life he had wrecked.

He owed Mickey Stanton more than an explanation.

He owed her freedom.

"Is it dark yet, honey" he asked.

She went to the window and glanced through the center crack in the drawn draperies. "Not quite, but it will be soon. Please, Johnny, let me call a doctor for you."

"I'm not sick. Not in any way that pills or medicines can cure." His face was grim. "I'm going to be my own doctor. I know what's wrong with me and I know the remedy. But I have to wait until the right time."

In spite of her worries, Mickey managed a wan smile. "Now you sound almost sinister. You know, like Dracula coming up out of his coffin at sundown."

It struck home. Nym Bardolph had buried him, but there was an hour when a ghost could rise and walk among the living. His weak grin matched Mickey's and he started to sit up on the couch. "What did you do with my shoes?"

"I put them in the closet. You came in all wild-eyed and crazy and just flopped there. You wouldn't even let me undress you or get you into bed. But I did take your shoes off, at least."

"Get them for me, will you?"

"Johnny, what for? You're not going out?"

"Yes."

"Just when you're beginning to feel better? Please, Johnny, I'll get all upset again."

Wearily, he slumped back on the couch. "All right, honey, I won't go yet. It's too early, anyway."

"Too early for what?"

He shrugged. "Just too early, that's all."

"Oh, you're so stubborn." A devilish little light suddenly flickered in the depths of her eyes. "Sure you're not sick?"

"I'm sure."

"Then let me see if I can't take some of that stubbornness out of you."

"Huh? What do you mean?"

"You'll find out." Slowly, as if she were were walking down a burlesque runway, she moved toward him. Her fingers toyed with the frilly bow at the throat of her flowing negligee.

His eyes widened. "No, Mickey. Not now."

"Hush. It will make you feel well and strong again."

Will it? he thought. Maybe, but he doubted it. There was only one thing that would ever make him well and strong again—and it wasn't time for that yet.

But Mickey seemed so eager, almost pathetic in her need of him. Did he have the right to deny her this? Did he have the right to deny her *anything?*

She seemed to sense his acquiescence. The bow at her neck came loose and the fragile garment fell open.

There was nothing underneath. Nothing but full breasts that projected gently from the graceful body which had brought him surcease from care many times over. Nothing but tender femininity that smelled of perfume and woman, mixed and blended beyond scientific analysis. Nothing but Mickey, hot-eyed, leaning over him to bathe away the dirt and the pain.

His face felt the velvety softness of her. His nostrils quivered and flared at the delectable fragrance. His hands reached and investigated, seeking, finding, stroking...

It was no good.

It was nothing.

Johnny Martel was a dead man lying in a tomb. Dead men did not make love.

Dead men went out into the dark, but not to make love. Not to give pleasure to pretty girls.

"I—I'm sorry, Mickey."

"What is it?"

"I don't know. I just don't know."

"I do." A gush of tears welled up from within her. "That woman—I don't know what she's done to you. But it's as if you were dead, Johnny. You're no good to anybody, except her—and maybe yourself."

"I know, honey, I know. Only now it's different. I'm no good to myself either, and as for her"—he spat the word out—"well, there's only one thing I can do for Nym Bardolph. And it isn't what you think it is."

"Johnny, you've got me so mixed up I don't even know what we're talking about. Have you gone crazy?"

"Crazy?"

"There's a look in your eyes. I—I—"

"No, Mickey, I haven't gone crazy. I think maybe I've just become sane again. A man has to make up his own mind. It's only when he lets a woman start making it up for him—that's when he has to think about whether or not he might be crazy." He pushed her away sadly, gently, and sat up again. "Only that's the time when he can't think at all..."

"I'm so worried about you."

"Don't be, honey. From now on I want you to worry about yourself. You've been getting the dirty end of the stick too long. It's about time you got a little happiness too."

"Johnny, you're all the happiness I need."

"When I'm like this?" He chuckled sardonically. "Half a man is worse than no man at all. And I'm not even half a man."

Her tear-stained face pleaded. "You're all the man I want. But she's taken you away from me." Anger seeped into her tones and she made a motion as if she were strangling a throat between her hands. "Oh, I could kill that woman. I could just *kill* her—"

Abruptly he broke into her display of emotion. "Get my shoes, Mickey."

"Don't go."

"Get my shoes." His voice was harsh.

Submissively, she went to the closet, found his shoes and brought them back. Dropping to her knees, she placed them before him and laced each one up as he slid a stockinged foot into it.

He stood up quickly. "Now kiss me."

Her mouth was ready, but there was little lust in his kiss. Instead, in an engulfing wave of sentiment they clung to each other tightly, holding on like frightened children in the teeth of an approaching storm.

"Johnny, Johnny..."

"Goodbye, honey."

"Goodbye? What do you mean? Johnny, you sound as if—"

His lips quieted her. "Don't worry, Mickey. Everything's going to be all right."

He walked out, leaving her standing there in unhappy bewilderment, a sweet girl lost in the muck that had poured down upon her. The muck that was his responsibility.

But Mickey had been right. Johnny was sick, sick in body and sick in mind. And so was the rest of the surrounding world. Everyone was sick—everyone who had ever been exposed to whatever horrible and contagious disease it was that Nym Bardolph was carrying.

But it was dark now, and he knew how to cure the sickness. Or at least how to keep it from spreading.

And after that—well, after that, what difference did it make?

CHAPTER TEN

Nym Bardolph stretched her slender, beautiful legs under the dashboard of the white Cadillac convertible. A sudden pain shot down her back, but she remained still, and dropping her head back on the cushion, she closed her eyes.

The dreadful bruises on her face could not hide the clean-cut, almost Grecian features.

It's over, she thought. It's done. Just as I always felt it would be done. It is complete, and the completion is a lovely thing—a thing I can touch with my thoughts and caress with the little fingers of my mind.

She wrapped her arms about herself and hugged her slim, elastic body within their compass. The pain shot through her again, but she did not mind. It made her truly know her triumph. It reminded her of what she had gone through to achieve it.

Never, never, never did I know that a woman could feel like this! It is the beginning. Now lies ahead the straight, unswerving road which will be easy to walk.

For now I am alone. Now nothing stands in my way.

For a brief second she thought of Sean, who had been part of her life. Who had been the ladder on which she climbed. But what about Sean? What about the things that might have been ... I married Sean for only one thing. *Revenge!*

Nym stirred restlessly. She searched her purse for a cigarette and finding none, she sat up straight, turned on the dashboard light, and searched the depths of the glove compartment, finally emerging with a pack of ancient smokes.

She tore open the wrapper and punching the dash lighter with a vicious movement, she waited impatiently until it got hot. Then she applied the glowing coil to the tip of a slightly bent cigarette. She pulled so deeply of the smoke that it seemed to permeate her body.

As she replaced the lighter she caught a glimpse of herself in the rear-view mirror. She leaned closer and examined her face. It was a ghastly, bruised sight. Both eyes were blackened and her lips were puffed and swollen. She smiled wryly and the smile hurt like the devil.

Suddenly she felt ravenously hungry but, looking at her face, she thought: I will wait a little while before going in. People are bound to stare. Perhaps if I wait a little, the dining room will be empty.

The soft dance music from the country club drifted out to her through the open terrace doors and the umbrella-like tops of the royal palms swayed ever so gently, as though in time to the tune.

Nym Bardolph, her face and body aching with her bruises, began to tremble. She ran her hands down over her full, pointed breasts, impeccably attired in the latest from the choicest of the most exclusive little shops in Miami. With wry amusement she thought of how ragged the underwear under the suit was, and why she was wearing it like that.

Alone, she thought. I am alone. Well, that's the way I want it.

She turned her head toward the brightly lighted building. Through the window she saw the dancers. The revelers. The Saturday night drunks.

I should be in there. I, of all of them, have something to celebrate.

But then she remembered that she was alone now. That she had nothing in common with them any more. Her eyes narrowed perceptibly under their puffed lids, and she took a deep, satisfied breath.

She moved away from the car in the soft moonlight and walked slowly out onto the golf course. She turned her back to the clubhouse deliberately.

She passed the first green without knowing where she was going or why. She just kept walking although it hurt her to walk. All about her in the shadows of the Florida night she was conscious of the gentle murmurings, the sweet soft laughter, the deeply caught breaths of the young Saturday-nighters engaged in that most secret and joyous part of life which is the birth-right of all.

If they want it.

Without knowing how she had gotten there, she found her feet sunk deeply in the softness of a sandtrap. She struggled irritably to extricate them from the sucking, slithering substance.

She never felt the bullet when it struck her squarely between the shoulder blades. The last impressions she had in this mortal life were two sounds—the giggle of a young girl behind some bushes to her right and the soft, smacking thud of the bullet as it entered her flesh.

Then she knew nothing more. Nothing more at all.

She neither saw nor heard nor felt the sobbing figure that fell across her form.

Nym Bardolph was very much alone.

There was a great crowd gathered about the sandtrap when they lifted the sobbing Johnny Martel from Nym's still body. Latecomers on the outside of the group asked the usual questions and those on the inside stared in horror at this sudden manifestation of death by violence.

When it comes suddenly—when death is not a daily occurrence—it is a difficult thing to grasp. When it happens to someone you have known all your life, it is a stunning thing which you deny with your mind even while your eyes see it.

None of the people in the crowd understood the death of Nym Bardolph. She had, perhaps, been a little ruthless in her business dealings. Lately, since Sean—whom they all knew well—had left, she had perhaps been a little indiscreet with Johnny Martel.

But that this could lead to murder ... to sudden violence and death ... was not to be understood.

And eventually Johnny, who had always been a good and gentle boy, was led away and Nym's body was carried off by men in white uniforms and driven to the undertaking parlor.

The crowd drifted back to the clubhouse.

And such is the unbelievability of death that soon the music started again and slowly, two by two, the dancers returned to the floor.

And after a while it was as if nothing had happened.

But five people out of all the citizens in Okeechee knew that something had happened and knew that they must live with it all their lives.

Lynn knew, and made a careful, painfully won decision. She must go somewhere else and start again.

And Sean knew. And such was his ironic fortune that the inheritance laws of Florida award all worldly goods of a person dead without a will to the spouse. Through the death of his wife, Sean regained all the property she had taken from him.

But one piece of property—eighteen acres to the north of town, including a most crucial fifty feet—he gave to the city, and such was the city's gratitude that the development they eventually put up, part of which was on the old Bardolph land, they called Bardolph Village in memory of the unfortunate young woman who unjustly met her death by an assassin's bullet.

And Michelle Stanton, known as Mickey, knew and it was two years before she had regained her equilibrium enough to marry Sean O'Sullivan and move with him into a new house which he had built as far from the golf course as possible.

And Mr. Frederick Gordon, known amongst his cronies as Tiny, knew. But there was nothing he could do.

And one more knew—Johnny Martel, who sat motionless in his cell and waited for what must inevitably come to him.

Yes, Johnny Martel knew.

And it was a bitter, bitter thing.

THE END

www.ingramcontent.com/pod-product-compliance
Lightning Source LLC
Chambersburg PA
CBHW030350180626
46812CB00007B/2827